FOUR VIEWS OF ME

© LUCIA FUDGE
2015

For Nina Rush and my Nina

Chapter 1

"It went away as silently as it came." Emily rubbed her abdomen as she spoke.

"What did?"

"My period. It stopped around August and I haven't had one since. After so many years, it feels odd not to have them. Like I've lost a part of my femininity."

"Lucky you, my mum had them until she was 60." Sue shuddered. "Just imagine, I'll be fertile for another decade! Could you imagine having a baby at our age?"

"I couldn't imagine having a pet, let alone anything else."

Emily sat on a high backed stool at the kitchen bench and traced the speckled pattern of Caesarstone. She watched as Sue walked around the lounge, opening cupboard doors and inspecting the floor tiles.

"Nice storage, Emms."

The smell of newness permeated the apartment; fresh paint and shiny floor tiles.

Sue came over to the bench and sat beside Emily. "I like it. You can keep it." She smiled. "I thought you'd put on weight recently. I put it down to the divorce; too many tim tams late at night, while sobbing into your hankies."

"Still the mean little bitch I knew in high school."

Emily walked across to the sliding door that opened onto her patio. She looked down at the cottage to her left. "She's there again."

"Who?"

"The old lady in the ramshackle cottage. My 3 o'clock Charlie."

"Where?"

"Far corner of the porch. Not much to her. See how shrivelled and fragile we'll be in 30 years time?"

"I'll botox my arms and legs before I look like that."

"You're good for another 10 years. Skin dries out when your period goes; lack of collagen and all that. I'll look mummified way before you."

"But your boobs are still perky. If mine go any further south, they'll be swimming with penguins in the Antarctic. Snake hips still looks 25 in the shade?"

"She has 500 gym memberships, just running around renewing them keeps her looking youthful."

"God bless her and all who sail in her."

"I'll drink to that."

"Speaking of which, what are we drinking? A girl could die of thirst in this hip bachelor pad."

"Three untruths in one sentence. That's a record, Suzie, even for you. This apartment is neither hip, nor a bachelor pad and you are definitely no girl."

"Ha ha."

Emily pressed her head against the glass door. "Do you remember at the end of year 7, you were getting your first period? I sat with you at lunch because you were having cramps."

"You looked after me so well, my mini mum."

"I didn't tell you that I already had my period for 6 months."

"No! I was such a drama queen and you were suffering in silence. Emily, you're too noble for your own good."

"Au contraire! I didn't get a single cramp the entire 38 years I had my period. I remember thinking how feminine you were, doubled over in a womanly mystery I was excluded from. I barely got hips or breasts for that matter, so I felt a total boy." She gave a short laugh. "And my period left with as little fanfare as it came. Story of my life."

"Bob left you with enough fanfare."

"True." Emily glanced down again. "Listen, she likes to play Puccini. La Boheme seem to be her favourite. I hear it late at night.

"You're starting to obsess about this old bird."

"No, I'm not." Emily turned away and studied her apartment. She liked examining where light fell on the bare white walls. The open plan lounge area was dominated by a two piece black leather sofa. The style was a nod to the Art Deco period, with chrome frame and sculptured sides. A lampshade with Asian motifs rested on a Chinese side cabinet. The stark white floor tiles were softened by several wool rugs.

Emily lay down on the sofa, gazed up at the ceiling and sighed.

"You ok? You're thinking of Bob."

"I'm thinking of how much I miss my old ceilings."

Sue laughed.

"These modern apartments lack soul. Cheaply designed and built for midgets. My old house was a glorious jumble of architraves, picture rails and plaster features."

"You were always complaining about the maintenance. Just think of the saving in paint bills."

"I miss it and all that went with it."

"Bob included?"

"Not yet. I'm still angry he left me for a high maintenance thirty eight year old. I felt guilty getting a facial, yet she spends a fortune freezing her face and he shells out like a lovesick teenager."

"She's two years off forty. You'll have the satisfaction of calling her the middle aged replacement in a couple of years."

"You're my tonic."

"Then can I ask you a personal question?"

Emily nodded.

Sue pointed to the floor. "Why?"

Neatly stacked against the wall were a large pile of paintings. Sunlight caught the mahogany frames and lit the wood. An ornate, antique mirror lay on its side and reflected the length of the room.

"I'm not ready to hang anything yet."

"But you gave Bob the antique furniture and all the china. I thought the lounge and rugs were your fresh start."

"These paintings are my memories. I can't hang them until this feels like home."

"Emms, the apartment's lovely; close to the city and to the shops.

Two bedrooms, so one of the kids can stay over but not both at the same time. Lots of restaurants nearby. And me."

Emily squeezed her hand. "I know. Last Friday, the first night I slept here, I put the key in the lock and opened the door. It was so silent, I heard the wall clock in the kitchen tick each second of my new life away. When the kids were little, Bob would fling the front door open when he arrived home at night. The kids would run to him, their feet pattering on the floorboards. That was only twenty years ago but it felt like an arid memory. I couldn't step inside, I had to go for a walk to calm my nerves."

"It'll pass. C'mon, I want my cup of tea."

Emily stood and walked slowly into the kitchen. She switched the sleek, black kettle on, its chrome spout nestled against the glass splash-back and slim-line white cabinets. She stared out the window at the streetscape below. Terraces and cottages lined the street, shrubs and fragrant flowers in the small front gardens.

"I've always loved Erskineville, but the kids will never be able to afford a house in the inner west now. Bob and I had talked about downsizing and giving both of them a deposit for a first home. There won't be much to inherit with snake hips so much younger than Bob."

"They can make their own way, Emms. You've given them a great education and a stable upbringing."

"Look how that turned out."

"Now you're being maudlin and there's no time for that."

"What is there time for?"

"A new life, Emms. New home, maybe a new man."

"I'm too bitter over the old man."

"Really?"

Emily hesitated.

"It wasn't the first time, was it?"

Emily stared at the ceiling again.

"What is it with ceilings and you?"

Emily laughed. "The first time I caught him playing around on me, I heard the racket he was making with his colleague in the attic. Remember my kids practised their music up there? Bob snuck this woman upstairs one Friday night while the kids were at a school recital. We came back early because Dominic felt sick. We came in so quietly Bob didn't hear us. I put the kids to bed and waited for him. I got more than I bargained for!"

"You never said anything to me. You confronted him, of course."

"I pretended I was asleep on the sofa. I was going to tell you, past tense. After the kids left home and I'd left him."

Sue was silent.

"Your silences are as noisy as ever."

"Would you really have left first?"

"That's unfair, Sue, you know I would."

Sue lifted a canvas bag from the floor. "I got you a housewarming present."

"Do people still buy such things?"

"Standards need to be maintained."

"Thanks." She eyed the parcel. "I guess it's not a throw rug or a cushion."

"I never give frivolous gifts."

"Because I'm a woman of worth and substance."

"Precisely. Now, open it."

"What on earth....."

"I knew you'd like it. Everyone needs a chalkboard in their kitchen. You can write mundane stuff on it, like grocery lists or something profound."

"Like what?"

"Like how's my bloody tea coming along?"

Emily reached into the cupboard. "Hope you're ok with herbal, I haven't done a grocery shop yet."

"I'd be ok with hot water and a cardboard cut out of a biscuit at this stage."

Chapter 2

The phone rang as Emily poured tea.

"God, that's the first time its rung! Hello."

"You sound breathless."

"Not at all, Bob. You're the first person to call me. I was just telling Sue."

"Is that bitch there?"

She put her hand over the receiver and mouthed. "He says hi."

Sue rolled her eyes as she accepted her tea. She eyed the brew in the mug. It looked like cat's pee.

"I was ringing to see if you're ok. You were upset when the removalists came to the old place."

"You mean my home, Bob. Yes, I was upset, I'd lived there twenty five years."

"You chose to sell at this time. We could have rented the house out for a couple of years until the market picked up."

"I needed stability; renting wouldn't give me that."

"You've always craved that. Elspeth has your settled gene. I could live in a cardboard box."

She listened.

"Emms, you won't get far if you spend much time with that woman. Make some new friends. Kids dropped by yet?"

"No."

"God, I wish they would, they're eating us out of hearth and home. I'll get onto them. Glad you're ok, Emmy."

"Don't call me th.."

"We should go out, all of us, so the kids feel comfortable with the situation. Sarah and Matt look to be pretty serious, there'll be some big occasions ahead for those two. You can bring a friend, I don't mind."

"Thanks, Bob."

"We've got to look out for each other. Bye Emmy."

Emily turned to face Sue. "He's calling from work."

"When's he going to retire?"

"He's only fifty five, he can go for another ten years."

"Advertising's a cruel business for someone his age."

"He and snake hips have bought a townhouse in Balmain, they borrowed quite a bit apparently. He can't afford to retire."

"How hip, mortgaged to the eyeballs in groovy Balmain. Just think of the dinner party chatter about whose repayments are the highest." Sue paused. "What will you do work wise?"

"I'll keep my bookkeeping job. I might work with morons but I'm not up for another change yet."

Emily wandered across to the window and glanced down at the cottage. "She's going inside now. I think she's got a dog, I hear it barking in the back garden. Hope I don't dress like that when I'm old."

"Personally, I hope I do. Clashing colours and eccentric patterns, maybe with a parrot on my shoulder and a tea cosy over my head. Something to look forward to in my dotage."

Sue took a sip of tea. "Yuck! Give me a piece of chalk."

She reached up to the chalkboard and wrote: "Chamomile tea looks like cat's pee and smells like old ladies' hankies. The taste is somewhere in between."

Emily laughed. "I'll hang that above the phone. My first work of art."

"That's the spirit, Emms. A new life. Who needs architraves?"

Chapter 3

"Watch out!"

Emily turned back sharply, to see a dog lunge past her on the footpath. An old woman stood behind her, watching the dog as it bounded ahead.

"I'll catch it for you," Emily called out. She ran along the footpath after the heedless dog. The dog increased its speed and distance from her and she paused to catch her breath. She glanced behind her at the woman. "She doesn't even look fazed," she marvelled.

Suddenly, a piercing whistle sounded. Emily watched as the large dog did an abrupt about face and ran back to its owner. It stopped and lay at her feet.

"Is that all I had to do?" She called out as she walked back.

"No sense in both of us running off like a two bob watch."

Emily laughed.

"Don't think I could? There was a time, not too long ago, when I could run across a paddock as fast as this old girl."

"What's her name?"

"Mimi."

"As in Puccini's Mimi? I hear it playing in your home; my balcony runs alongside your front garden. La Boheme is one of my favourite operas."

"That man understood tragedy." The nut brown face assessed Emily as she spoke.

A ring of interlinking circles criss-crossed her forehead and cheeks. They encircled her eyes, giving her the appearance of an aged circus clown. A thick, matted head of white hair complimented her sharp features.

"You're staring at me."

"I am. Sorry." Emily held out her hand. "I'm Emily Sargent. I've just moved into the apartment complex next door."

"That hideous monstrosity? I campaigned against it, had the whole street on my side. You never know who lives in a high rise block.

Your local axe murderer could easily hide within."

"It's only 3 storeys high and I haven't met any psychos. Yet."
"Hmm."
"I didn't catch your name."
The woman stood straight and held out a steady hand. "Sylvia Baker."
"What a lovely name! You don't hear it any more."
"They broke the mould with me. Some of my friends said it was for the best."
For the first time, Sylvia smiled and Emily watched as the circles pulled in different directions.
Mimi whined.
"Wait for the signal, old girl." Sylvia whistled and Mimi darted down the street again.
Sylvia swayed on her feet as Mimi brushed past her.
Emily put a hand out to steady her but Sylvia brushed her away.
"I can manage."
"I'm sorry, I didn't mean to offend you."

Emily watched as Mimi disappeared down the street. "So how far do you walk her?"
"Watch me." Sylvia squinted as she watched the dog's progress. As she neared the intersection ahead, she whistled again and the dog ran back.
Emily laughed. "One street?"
"Works for us. Mimi's a good dog, she always comes back. Makes me think she must be part cattle dog."
"How long have you done this routine?"
"A good 3 years, since my hip replacement. Don't grow old, my girl, that's my advice."
"I've haven't been called a girl in thirty years. Thank you."
"A turn of phrase. You look like you belong somewhere else, not here."
Emily looked away as she spoke. "I'm divorced, two months ago."

"You can tell you're not a country girl."

"Pardon?"

"City girls always watch their words. I noticed that when I moved to Sydney during the war. Drove me mad trying to have a conversation, always so careful saying what they thought. I felt like I was playing chess blindfolded."

A mischievous light lit Sylvia's eyes.

"How old were you when you moved to Sydney?"

"Eighteen. Fresh out of secretarial school and desperate to see all the excitement of the town. My best friend lived on a prosperous farm and she holidayed every Christmas in Sydney. Her stories of trams, ships in the harbour and dances at the Rocks filled me with awe."

"Did it meet your expectations?"

"Yes and no." Sylvia moved stiffly from side to side. "Damn hip, locks up on me if I stand for too long." She motioned to her front gate. "If we're going to have a yarn, might as well sit and be comfortable while we're at it."

"Sorry, I can't stay. I need to get basic food supplies or I'll be chewing my furniture for dinner. Another time, definitely."

"You apologise too much. Three times in the space of five minutes."

Emily was silent.

"Very well." Sylvia whistled and Mimi jumped to her feet and bounded off again. "That's my girl, off you go."

Emily realised Sylvia was speaking to her dog and not to her.

"Goodbye, I'm sure we'll meet again."

Sylvia nodded, her eyes focussed on Mimi.

Emily thought a smile lurked in her eyes.

Chapter 4

"He was a deadshit of a kid."

"Sarah!"

"It's true, Mum. You can't say anything bad about anyone."

"I don't want to say anything bad about my own son."

Sarah held her gaze. "Remember the puppy he got for Christmas? It bit him on the leg and he never went near it again. He throws things away, as if they have no value. He treated Jenny the same way, she lost her value when she got a higher paying job than him."

"I'm sure the reason they broke up was more complicated than that."

"I wish." Sarah perched on the arm of the sofa and Emily watched as her eyes appraised the lounge room.

"You think it's too small?"

"It's fine." Sarah brought her calm gaze back to her mother. "It's just different to our old place. I didn't think I'd care when you and Dad sold up in Strathfield because I'd been gone for five years. But I did. Even Dom said it made him feel like an orphan not having a family home anymore. The little deadshit."

Emily laughed. "You need to find a new expletive for him, that one's getting a little old."

"What's old is Dom running back to you because Jenny left him. He can find a flatmate to share with, you deserve some time on your own."

"I'd quite like some company. For a while."

"As long as it doesn't turn into servitude for you. Dad treated you like crap, I don't want it to happen again." Sarah shrugged her shoulders and her blonde hair fell forward, catching the sunlight.

"She still looks like a Botticelli angel," Emily mused, "even when she's telling me off."

She moved across to a stool at the kitchen bench. "I deserve a change of conversation. What's new with you?"

"Matt and I are thinking of trying for a baby this year."

"What! Aren't you a bit young?"

"I look at some of the teachers I work with. Some are in their late thirties and trying for their first child. Matt's finished his Masters and he's earning good money. We think it's a good time. My career is family friendly."

"What about buying your own place? Doesn't that come first?"

"Not for us."

"And marriage?"

"We're committed to each other. I don't need a ring to feel married."

"You might when you're at home with a baby, isolated from work life and not feeling as secure as you did in your old life."

"Maybe that's how you felt back then, but I'm not you. Matt suggested it but I said no. The ring's just a ritual. All that counts is that we love each other."

"You're leaving yourself wide open for heartbreak if you have that attitude."

"A ring didn't protect you very well, did it? It's a symbol, nothing more. I won't be anyone's chattel."

"I don't think I was."

"Sorry, Mum. I'm edgy at the moment. All this change is freaking me out. Seeing the apartment set me off, I know how much you loved our old place. I've bitten your ear off all afternoon and you haven't said a word."

Sarah's mobile rang and she sprang up to take the call on the balcony. She slid the glass door open and the sound of Puccini sounded from Sylvia's house.

"She likes it loud." Emily thought.

She swivelled on her stool and examined the room. The flat had started to make itself known to her. A newborn creature of light and shadows, lit with easterly sun in the morning. By mid afternoon, the lounge was ablaze in yellow light. By late afternoon, shadows fell across the walls.

The quiet patterns of suburbia intrigued her. She sat on her balcony early each morning, a take away cappuccino in hand and watched people walk to Erskineville station. She devoured her copy of the Daily Telegraph as she sat. "Bob would be appalled," she mused, "only the Australian will do for him."

She hadn't made a coffee since Sue's visit. Neither had she cooked a meal. "Perfectly good take away down the road," she reasoned, "I've cooked enough meals over the years. Time for a break."

She glanced at the frames on the floor and visualised them on the walls. "Not yet," she thought.

She watched Sarah as she chatted to Matt on her mobile, her face animated as she she described a workmate to Matt and her warm laugh rang out. Sarah leaned over the railing and her back stiffened. "He's here," she said in a low voice, "I'll talk later."

Emily watched as she re-entered the room.

"I just saw Dom's car pull up."

"Lovely, he hasn't seen the place furnished."

The buzzer sounded and Sarah moved across to the intercom. "Come on up. I'll leave the door open."

Emily felt the twinge of nerves again, as she settled in an armchair.

"Hey bro. Welcome to Mum's new pad."

Dominic's long, angular body hunched over to kiss Emily.

"Greetings, abandoned mother."

"Darling, how are you?" Emily felt the dry touch of his embrace.

"You've gone all out with customising your space, I see."

"I've only been here a month."

"A sofa's good. It's all I need."

Sarah interrupted. "You can't commit to more than one piece of furniture, Dom."

"Unlike you, Ikea princess."

Emily listened. "All that music tuition paid off," she mused, "they spar with such delicate execution."

"Tea anyone?"

Dominic flopped onto the couch. "You can't afford alcohol, Mum?"
Sarah nudged him. "Don't give her a hard time. Is Jenny ok?"
"No. I'm unforgettable."
"I'm going, Mum. Matt's meeting me at Newtown for drinks."
"Don't leave on my behalf, Sar."
"As if."

Sarah tripped as she bent to collect her handbag from the edge of the sofa. Then she moved the picture frames closer to the wall. "Mum, hang those things! They're a hazard."
"I will, darling. Thanks for stopping over."
"It's the pot plants all over again." Sarah muttered to Dominic as she straightened up. "You watch, it'll happen again." She strode across the room and waved a hand as she left. " Don't get up, Dom."
"As if."
Emily glanced across as he spoke. "He looks thinner." She thought. His dark brown eyes were half closed in the twilight. Light faded in the room and she reached across for the lamp.
"Do you miss it?"
She started at the words. "I thought you were falling asleep."
"In your company? Never. Do you miss it?"
"The house?"
"All of it. Us together, Dad, your home."
Emily sat in silence awhile.
"And you, do you miss her?"
They had dialogued like this for years. Each engaged in their thoughts, sentences unanswered and replies unexpected. No Sarah to give direct answers.
The twilight descended into darkness as they sat. Perfectly silent in their conversation.

Chapter 5

"Sue, you've called me to tell me that you're too busy to talk?"

"I didn't say that!"

"You just did a minute ago. Everything ok, you haven't been retrenched or transferred?"

"Look, I'm busy now." She laughed. "My God, I really did say that, Emms."

"Twice."

"I got an irregular pap smear result about a fortnight ago."

Emily sat upright. "What does that mean?"

"It means I have to see a gynaecologist to have my girlie bits checked out further."

"And you waited till now to tell me?"

"You've been mooching about in your apartment, looking heartbroken. And there's nothing to say until I see my gyno tomorrow afternoon." A pause. "Will you come with me?"

"Absolutely. As long as I don't have to see anything, I'm your man."

"Thank you. I'll email the details over. Must go, I've got two people waiting outside my door."

"You called me, remember?"

"I'm busy, bye."

Emily hung up the phone and perched on a stool. The call unsettled her and she glanced at the chalkboard, eyeing the chalk on the bench in front of her. "I've no witticisms or profound comments on my new life." she mused. "Same old, same old." She walked across to the sliding door and moved onto the balcony.

An bark sounded and she spied Mimi and Sylvia on the pavement outside. Mimi shook with excitement as Sylvia held a tennis ball. "Fetch, girl." She raised her hand and Mimi crouched, tiger-like, for the moment. The ball slipped out of her hand and fell away onto the road.

"No, Mimi, stop! I'll get it." Sylvia shouted as the dog ran across the road, oblivious to the traffic.

Emily gasped and ran from her apartment. She charged down the stairs and ran onto the pathway, shouting.

"Don't move, Sylvia! I'll get her."

"Save her." Sylvia clutched her arm. "My dog's somewhere on the road. I can't see her."

Car brakes slammed hard on the street.

"It's ok, Sylvia." Emily rushed out and searched the road. Mimi padded up the centre of the road, tennis ball clutched inside her drooling jaws. A car horn tooted and Emily waved at the driver.

"Hey lady, train your dog. This isn't Centennial Park, you dickhead."

"Charming language, I presume you'd speak to your mother like that?"

"She isn't a dickhead." He took off and Emily contemplated giving him the finger.

Mimi dropped the ball at Emily's feet.

"I'm not picking that up. Mimi, come on, you finish the job."

The dog walked back to Sylvia as the ball rolled into the gutter.

Another motorist tooted their horn as they passed and she shouted. "It's not my dog." She kicked the ball onto the pavement.

Sylvia clutched Mimi's collar and crouched as low as she could to her. "Sorry, my girl. What a foolish thing to do to you."

Emily noticed the pallor of her skin and that her hands shook as she stroked the dog. She focussed her eyes as Emily approached. "Oh, it's you! My knight in middle aged armour. Thank you. I do hate asking for help but I really needed you." She moved slowly to her front gate. "Mimi, I've had enough for one afternoon. You'll have to walk twice as long tomorrow."

"Your ball," Emily called out, "you forgot the ball."

Slyvia walked on and Emily grimaced as she picked up the slimy ball. "Always the bunny." She thought. She eyed the retreating figure of Sylvia as she walked up the pathway. She flung the ball over the gate to a corner of the garden, where it landed harmlessly. Mimi's ears pricked up at the sound but Sylvia kept a firm hand on her collar.

Emily rinsed her hands at the outdoor tap. She could hear Sylvia murmuring to Mimi from the front porch and the dog's disappointed whines as she thumped the porch with her tail. "Not today, girl, I'm too shaky."

Emily's heart tugged at the words.

She moved across to the outdoor garden at the front of her complex and sat on a wooden bench, set back from the lawn. Small conifers, of equal size and distance from each other, lined the garden beds. "I bet the spacing is accurate to the centimetre," she mused. "It looks like they were planted by a mathematician." She stared at the plantings. "Too many neat lines in my life." She thought. "Is this how I'll see out my days? A withered divorcee living in a clinically maintained complex?" She stood.

"Are you still there?" A gnarled hand clutched the low fence that separated the two dwellings.

"Yes, Sylvia, I'm just catching my breath. That frightened the life out of me."

"And me. I take afternoon tea in fifteen minutes. If you're not grocery shopping, would you care to join us?"

"Love to. I'll pick something up from the bakery."

"Not too sweet. Mimi loves a plain croissant."

Emily rolled her eyes as she turned away. "First I nearly get bloody run over saving the dog," she thought, "then I'm buying it afternoon tea. I'm mad."

She crossed the road and headed to the bakery. A gentle wind lifted foliage and shook flowers, releasing fragrance in its wake. Emily admired the restored cottages she passed as she walked on. She stopped to smell a gardenia tree and picked a few fallen flowers from the pathway, tucked them inside her hand. "A bouquet for Mimi," she mused, "just to complete the absurdity of my afternoon." She approached the end of the block and stopped at the last terrace.

"I can't believe it!" She looked upwards. "How did I not notice it before?"

She stared at the two storey terrace and the hairs on the back of her arms stood up. A tug of her heart kept her motionless.

It was painted the same colour scheme as her old home in Strathfield. A discoloured, white exterior with green shutters and mahogany trim. Emily peered into the open window upstairs and spied an ornate, white washed ceiling, heavy with plaster features and wide architraves. She turned away from the terrace and wiped her eyes.

The magnolias lay crushed in her hands. She dropped them and hurriedly made her way to the bakery. The white petals lay on the roadside, abandoned to chance.

Chapter 6

"Come in, my girl. Nothing friendlier than a whistling kettle."

"Or a stranger bearing gifts." Emily wiped her feet on the front mat.

"This is an extraordinary day for me."

Emily noticed the tremor in Sylvia's voice as she spoke.

"I need to ask for your help again. I can't carry the tray to the porch. Most days I manage on my own. If I'm not so steady on my feet, I have tea inside, but it's so much nicer outside."

Emily followed her down a spacious, central hallway to a small, whitewashed kitchen at the end of the passage. A 1950's kitchen in well preserved state presented to her. A ledge above a disused chimney housed assorted bric-a-brac and plastic containers. Pale yellow cupboards lined the walls, with faded green knobs. Stained linoleum flooring underfoot. A worn chintz curtain at the window blew in a summer breeze.

"Let's go, then." Emily lifted the tray and carried it to the front porch as Sylvia followed behind her.

They sat and Sylvia poured the tea into fine china cups. "My mother was most particular about her tea," she observed as she handed Emily a cup. "She said that during the war, it was impossible to get good tea because of the rationing. Said her first cup after the restrictions eased was the most satisfying of her life. Have you ever had that feeling?"

"My first ironing session after my ex-husband, Bob, moved out. No pin-striped business shirts to iron or trousers to press to perfection. I hoped his new girlfriend refused to do them. Or burnt them attempting it."

"That's an unexpected bit of backbone coming from you."

"That's great coming from you, when I nearly got myself killed chasing after your dog."

"Touche'. There's lemon and sugar on the tray. Tea's so refreshing with lemon."

"Why don't you have someone walk Mimi for you? School kids will walk her for a pittance. You could advertise in the local paper."

"One of my mates from bowls got a dog walker and she was robbed two weeks later. Ended up in hospital with a broken arm. No, we'll carry on as we are, thank you."

Sylvia whistled and Mimi's ears pricked up. The dog placed her head squarely on Sylvia's lap and drooled as a croissant was broken up and held out to her. Emily watched as saliva and crumbs gathered on Sylvia's lap, as Mimi devoured the treat.

"You must be appalled by this." Sylvia caught her eye.

"Not at all. My kids did it all the time with our dog."

"You lost it in the divorce?"

"No, he died two years ago."

"How sad for you."

"I get hay-fever and Gus drove me crazy dropping fur everywhere. I sneeze a lot less now. And vacuum less. I'm sorry if that makes me sound heartless."

Late afternoon sun lit the porch.

Emily studied Sylvia. She resembled an aged hawk, her silver hair crowning her sharp eyes and pert nose. She bent her head to sip her tea and Emily watched as myriad lines swallowed her lips and cheeks.

"Your lot have complained about me."

"Pardon?"

"Your Body Corporate. They've said that my dog and my music constitute noise pollution. Can you believe that? How could anyone call Puccini noise pollution?"

"I'm sorry to hear that. The walls are pretty thin, I can hear my neighbour's early morning pee. I call it the urinary orchestra."

Sylvia's lips stretched into a thin smile. "I know your type. A few middle aged ladies have come knocking at my door over the years, offering help. Did I need a lift to church? To the grocery shop? I told them I was square with God and my diet of canned soup. They stopped coming after that."

"You scared them away. You can look quite fierce, Sylvia."

"I hate to look helpless. Don't you?"

"I've never thought about it."

"Means you've never had to. Wait another thirty years and you'll see what I mean."

"Oh, I'll say yes to all the middle aged matrons offering help. I know my daughter won't be on my doorstep."

"Don't get on?"

"Mostly from a distance. Sarah's very opinionated and thinks our family's dysfunctional. Only she has a sane take on life." Emily crunched on a biscuit. "She could be right."

Sylvia was silent and Emily glanced about the porch.

A small cane table setting with four chairs was positioned near the doorway. A patterned jug held a posy of flowers gathered from the garden. A lifetime collection of pots littered the floorboards, from vintage 1950's shapes to modern terracotta pots. Within each, flowers and shrubs jostled for space.

"It's nice out here. How long have you lived here?"

"Sixty years. John Edward and I saved for four years for a deposit."

"Did you have a family?"

"No." Sylvia fingered a silver necklace as she spoke. "The Lord said no and no it was. I found other ways to serve. John Edward agreed with me."

"Did you always call your husband by two names?"

"His mother named him John after the Apostle and Edward after the King. Sad how that worked out, wasn't it?" Sylvia traced the intricate patterns of the locket that hung from her necklace as she spoke.

"Where did you live before Sydney?"

"Yalinda, a small settlement outside Adaminaby. The old township, that is, not the new one. Old Adaminaby was flooded during the Snowy Mountain Hydro Electric Scheme."

"How sad for you."

Sylvia brushed the crumbs from her lap. "Not really, I'd been gone 12 years. They moved most of the township in '57. My parents weren't affected, they were on land higher up."

Sylvia's eyes were unreadable. "I came to Sydney in 1945, just before the war ended."

"How old ..."

"How polite you are. City girl all your life?"

Emily nodded.

"My bowls partners were all from the big smoke. Nice ladies too. Oh, one was from Bowral but we don't class that as country."

"No indeed, I never have either. Too many middle aged matrons in expensive cars milling about."

"Touche, again." Sylvia's eyes registered amusement. "As I was saying, I was 18 years old and I'd never spent a single night in a big town. Just Yass at show time."

"Very brave of you, to leave your family behind."

"I was moving to start a life with John Edward. He'd proposed and I was eager to meet him when he came ashore. Mum approved, she did the same when Dad returned from the Great War."

Mimi lay her head on Sylvia's feet and she bent to caress him as she spoke. "Poor girl" she murmured, "she's longing for a proper run. Three years she's waited for me to take her to the park."

Mimi's tail thumped the floor in agreement.

"You have too much time on your hands, you've admitted as much to me. Silly to be locked in that concrete box while the day is fresh and new outside."

Emily looked down to hide a smile.

"I'll ask you a question and you can have a week to think about it."

"Go on."

"I want you to walk Mimi for me, two or three times a week."

"What!"

"I can trust you, my girl. You're steady and kind, though a bit door-matish for my taste."

"My sinuses and hay-fever?"

"Will be better for confronting them head on. It's the only way to tackle life."

"Look, I'm sorry. I work part time and I have two kids..."

"Multi tasking, apparently we women are brilliant at it. I can't pay you but I do have some lovely Decca records I can lend you and my opera glasses. Drop by next week and tell me your decision."

"Look, I'm sorry but ..."

Sylvia stood and stacked the tray. "I've enjoyed our tea. Next time we chat, I'll tell you more about John Edward." She pointed to the tray. "Would you?"

Emily lifted the tray and carried it into the hallway. The potent smell of aged wood as she walked the length of the corridor. She left the tray on the kitchen sink and exited the house.

"By the way, you apologised to me twice just now. I can see you are a professional apologist. We'll have to work on that. Thank you for saving Mimi, I'm so grateful." Sylvia smiled as Emily let herself out of the front gate. She turned to wave, then ran to her complex.

"How perfectly absurd!" she muttered to herself. "This could only happen to me. Why does this servitude follow me everywhere?" She stepped over the manicured buffalo grass, fighting a desire to scuff it with her shoes.

She let herself into the apartment and her eyes fell on the chalkboard. She wiped Sue's message away and wrote: "Never take tea with the devil. She always wins."

Chapter 7

"I couldn't say no."

"The hell you couldn't." Sue stared at Emily, who stood panting in the driveway, in sweat soaked clothes.

"Who owns that slobbering creature?"

"The old lady next door, the one I pointed out to you."

"Oh my God, it's happened. You're stalking her!"

"What a thing to say. We've become friends and she approached me about it."

"Sounds like you're substituting a problematic man for a problematic pensioner."

"Stop grumbling. I'll return Mimi and get ready. You're early, after all."

"I'm always early, you know that. And you're always rescuing people."

"You included?"

"If I were any more together, I'd run the universe for God."

"A God reference. Today must be a red letter day."

"You have fifteen minutes. I'll leave if you're not ready."

"Are you threatening me with missing out on hearing a specialist talk about your fanny?"

Sue walked across to the outdoor seat in the complex. "I'll wait here." She glanced about at the garden beds. "Do they vacuum out here? I've never seen such pristine surroundings. Complex must be run by ex cleaners." She pulled a novel out of her handbag and settled in for a read.

…..........................

"Why exactly are you seeing a gynaecologist today?"

Sue tapped the steering wheel with her hand as they waited in traffic on King Street.

"Last year, my doc noticed some changes in my cervix. She said she'd monitor my next pap smear. Well, she did and the cells are still changing. Apparently, they're considered pre-cancerous."

"Holy cow!"

"Who says that nowadays?" Sue slammed on the horn as a car cut in front of her.

"You didn't say anything about it last year."

"Emms, you were going through a divorce, Bob was pressuring you to rent the house and he moved in with snake hips. Do you think I'd drop another bomb on you?"

"I was so stressed, one more thing wouldn't have made much difference."

"Bloody pedestrians, they make roads for cars, not you morons! Get out of my way." Sue gestured to a young man who ambled across a set of green traffic lights.

He waved to her.

"Attitude to boot! Why are there so many cretins in the world?

Emily squeezed her arm. "He's probably a uni student, they all live in a parallel universe."

Sue straightened her back. "I'm dreading the examination. God knows what the instruments will be like."

"A foot long drill with spikes."

"There's no need to frighten me." Sue was laughing now as she pulled into a car park. "I've never been so sorry to arrive somewhere on time."

The waiting area was minimalistic, stark white leather lounges and coffee tables. Toddlers played on the floor, their young mothers sweeping several off the pristine couches as they attempted to clamber up.

Sue tapped her foot as she sat in an armchair. The magazine on her lap slid to the floor and she nearly bumped heads with Emily as they both bent to retrieve it.

"Do you need to sit on the floor and play with some Lego?" Emily whispered to her.

"I think I do."

At the end of a long corridor, a glossy black painted door opened and a spectacular sight met their eyes.

A thickset man with cropped, white hair approached the reception desk.

"Ms Smith?"

Sue stood and the magazine fell to the floor again. She gave it a kick and it skidded under the armchair, landing with a thud against the wall.

"Yes."

"I'm John Griffith. Please come through."

She exchanged a glance with Emily as they followed behind him. He wore tartan pants, a red shirt and black braces.

Emily whispered. "I'm glad it's your fanny he's checking and not mine."

Dr Griffith motioned to the chairs near his desk. "The first question I need to ask you is obvious. Sue Smith, is that an alias?" His lopsided grin added to his eccentric appearance.

Sue replied. "My mother used her entire reserves of wit in naming me, because she never did anything faintly amusing after that."

"Well, you've made it to fifty on that handle, so it must've been character forming. You're obviously made of stern stuff."

"I am but this examination scares me shitless."

"Probably not an outcome I'd like to see."

He leaned forward. "I've read your GP's notes and I do need to check you for the abnormalities detected in your pap smear. What I propose to do is a colposcopy, with an instrument like a large microscope. I use the same speculum your GP used in the pap smear to get a magnified view of your cervix. If you like, your, ah, friend can watch the results on the screen. The only thing I don't have is popcorn."

"Where's my head! I didn't introduce you. Dr Griffith, this is Emily, my best friend from high school."

Emily nodded. "Sue's always incoherent when she's nervous." She turned to Sue. "Do you want me there?"

"Just stand beside me, please. No peeking."

"That won't be hard."

"Follow me, ladies."

They walked into a small, high-tech room.

"This is the colposcope, it'll enable me to clearly identify any changes to the cells of your cervix. No, take them off. That's it, hop up there. Excellent. Ok, a little discomfort here, try to relax. Remember to breathe, then exhale. That's it, another breath." He was silent for a minute and Emily checked the screen.

"Does it look OK?"

"I can see why Sarah was concerned. There are some changes but they need further testing. What I'd like to do, Sue, is take a biopsy. I'm going to take a small sample of tissue from the cervix and send it to a lab for examination. The results will be back next week, so I want you to book an appointment for next Friday."

"And the results will show if the abnormalities are cancerous?"

"Precisely. You've had frequent pap smears in the past, so a diagnosis will give us a clearer picture. From there, we can decide the best course of action."

"Will you have to remove my girlie bits?"

"Too soon to say. A cone biopsy may be all you need, which treats very small tumours."

He turned away to the bench behind him and Emily leaned over to Sue. "Here comes the spiky drill."

"Who invited you?"

"You did."

Dr Griffith smiled down at Sue. "A couple of deep breaths, very good. I know it's uncomfortable, nearly there. Done." He turned back to the bench, speculum in hand. "I'll label these and have them sent off today. Come back to the office when you're changed."

Emily turned away as Sue dressed herself.

Sue muttered. "That wasn't too bad."

"Want to do it again?"

"You first."

Dr Griffith looked up as they re-entered the room. "I should start a series of questions regarding your diet and exercise regime but you look in great shape. I trust you have a healthy lifestyle, with exercise and a balanced diet?"

"I could improve on a few things." Emily snorted.

"Don't put your body through any extreme changes. Everything in moderation."

"Absolutely." Sue leaned forward. "Do you think it's cancerous?"

"You've been diligent in your previous testing. We have excellent treatment for early cancers. I wouldn't focus too much on the first consultation. We'll get the results and if need be, have a longer consult next week."

"Good call. I can arrange my diary around next Friday."

"Late or early is fine. I run a flexible schedule."

Sue turned to Emily. "Are you available next week?"

"No, I promised Dom I'd help him move in."

"He's coming back! This is the third time."

"He and Jenny split up. He's finding the empty space unnerving."

"I see." Sue turned to Dr Griffiths. "Hopefully, our next consult will be brief, no offence to you."

He smiled and she leaned forward. "Do you ever wear tartan green?"

"Not my best colour, unfortunately. Makes me look consumptive, which can unsettle my patients." He stood and shook her hand. "Again, try not to focus on today. Keep healthy and positive."

Emily waited as Sue settled her account at reception. She observed Sue's head tilt in conversation.

"I've never noticed that before," she mused, "has she done that ever since I've known her?"

Chapter 8

"Dom, I thought you were bringing just a few cases."

"The lease was up next month, so I gave notice. I'll look for something soon, Mum. I just need a bedsit."

"I'm not sure about that." Emily glanced about the lounge room. "Lucky my garage could fit your furniture." She stared at the garbage bags that littered the floor. "Can you move this stuff into the spare room?"

"I'll pack it away tomorrow, I'm too stuffed now. Just chill."

"I find it hard to chill in a pigsty." Emily sat at the end of the sofa and automatically swung a garbage bag at her feet to one side. "Hear the music? That's Sylvia playing her records. She showed me her record collection, all in mint condition. Old Decca recordings of Maria Callas and Joan Sutherland. It's some collection, tickets from the year the Sydney Opera House opened. She and John Edward loved to go to the Winter season. She even has tickets from La Scala from the 1960's."

"She should have it catalogued."

"She'd think I was making fun of her if I said that."

Emily visualised her sitting at the kitchen table, sipping tea and watching the breeze flutter through her curtains. "What does she think back to?" she wondered.

She stood and glanced at the hallway. "Dom, you must move all these bags into the spare room by tonight, they're a hazard."

"All in good time. What should we do for dinner? Maybe go to the Thai restaurant. I want to thank you somehow."

"Save your pennies. I'll make a casserole. I've been wanting to baptise the kitchen for the last six weeks."

"Thanks, I'm a bit short of funds at the moment. Want any help?"

"No, stay there. It won't take long."

"OK." He switched the TV remote on and lay on the sofa.

Emily examined the vegetable trays in her fridge. "Six

weeks," she thought, "I had no encumbrances for six whole weeks. I knew one of them would come running back."

The phone rang and she glanced across at Dominic. He was still prone on the sofa.

"Dom, please get that."

He didn't move.

She leaned across and lifted the receiver. "Hello."

"Emmy."

She gritted her teeth.

"Is Dominic there?"

"Just moved in today, Bob. Do you want to speak to him?"

"I just wanted to know he's with you. We saw him last weekend, he's pretty cut up about that bitch."

"Jenny, you mean." She watched as Dominic cocked his head at the name.

"She treated him shabbily."

Emily poured olive oil into a pan while she listened. She watched the movement of the oil as it slid around the sides of the pan. "Just like Bob," she thought, "slippery to the touch."

"It's good you can take him in. Elspeth's family is over from England and we couldn't empty the study, she was freaking out. We've so much stuff in the spare room as it is."

"Mm."

"You there, Emmy? So you still have the teak oil for cleaning the antiques? You do? Well, if you don't need it for your stuff, can you give it to Dominic and he can drop it off to us."

"You can't afford to buy a tin?"

"You don't need it anymore, with your glass and leather. Silly to waste the tin, isn't it? We might as well help each other out."

She was silent.

"Anyway, thanks for taking Dom in. Have you settled into the flat?"

"I have, I've met a lovely neighbour..."

He cut in. "Excellent. Gotta go, Emmy, we're taking the family out for dinner. Don't forget the oil."

The click sounded in her ear.

"Not my family," she thought, "you've moved on from that."

"What was Dad saying?"

"He's concerned about you."

"Not concerned enough to put me up for a while."

"Did you ask him?"

Dominic nodded as he leaned over to the fruit bowl and took an apple.

The phone rang and he said languidly. "Will I get that?"

"No, I'm closer." Emily picked the phone up, propped it against her ear as she threw garlic into the sizzling oil.

"Mum, it's me."

"Darling! You've caught me cooking my first proper meal in the kitchen. Cheese on toast doesn't count."

"I guess Dom's lying on the couch, sharpening his knife and fork as we speak."

"Not at all. All OK, darling?"

"Don't say anything to Dom. I've missed my period."

Emily dropped her ladle.

"Mum?"

"I guess you don't mean period at school?"

"Ha ha. No, I'm two days overdue."

"Any symptoms?"

"None at all but I'm never late. I'm not taking a test until Friday, so I won't get disappointed if my period comes before then. I've been told those pink line tests can really do your head in."

Emily was silent.

"Mum, I know you can't talk but are you pleased?"

"We don't know anything yet, but if you are, then naturally I am too."

"Thanks. Please don't say a word to him." Sarah laughed. "There's nothing to say yet."

"Sarah...."

"Don't worry, I'm fine. I'll call you later this week."

Emily stared at the blackened garlic in the saucepan. "That's it, we're having cheese on toast."

"Sarah OK?"

"As ever. Camembert or cheddar?"

The phone rang again and she slammed her ladle down as she reached to pick up the receiver again. "Yes?"

"Whoa, I can tell Dominic's back home."

"Not at all, Sue. You're my third call in a row."

"Nice to be so popular. I only get calls from receptionists."

"Any news?"

"I saw Dr Griffiths today. Not great news."

"Oh, Sue! Did he give you any options?"

"He recommended a surgical procedure and some form of chemo." Sue's voice faltered and Emily's throat constricted at the sound.

"It's early stages and the prognosis is very good nowadays."

"Do you want to pop round? We're having supper."

"Only dinosaurs have supper. I'm on my third glass of red wine, prepping for surgery."

"It's a grape based chemotherapy?"

Sue snorted. "Thanks for coming last Friday, I really need you."

"As if I wouldn't. Lots of veggies and fruit for you, not just the fermented ones."

"Don't lecture me. Save it for that wastrel son of yours."

"Is that necessary?"

"He plays you like a violin. Guess you're cooking and he's relaxing?"

"Have you been talking to Sarah?"

"Night, Emms."

Emily moved across to the fridge and stared at the cheese compartment.

"Mum, you ok?"

She started. "Lost in my thoughts. You know what, we're having take away tonight. Set two plates, I'll be back soon."

"I'll shout the next one. Can you leave me your mobile, I'm out of credit on mine. I gave Jenny your number in case she needed to call me."

Emily searched her pocket. She moved around the bench top and stumbled over a garbage bag. "That's it! They need to go away tonight." She handed Dominic her eftpos card. "You get the food, I'll clear the bags away. My pin number is my year of birth."

He lifted an eyebrow.

"Really, Dom! 1964. How can you not know that?"

He shrugged. "Details."

She watched as he negotiated the bags on the floor with his long legs. She cleared the floor immediately in front of the sofa and looked back at the kitchen. The chalkboard was wiped clean and she walked across to it.

"My new life," she wrote, "dog walker, single mother and friend. Enough for now."

She turned back to the lounge and continued carrying garbage bags to the spare room. The familiar cleaning routine soothed her disquieted heart.

Chapter 9

"Don't you trust me?"

Sylvia stared at Emily. "What an extraordinary thing to ask me. Would I entrust Mimi to you if I didn't?"

Emily drummed her fingers on the kitchen table. "Then why won't you come for afternoon tea to my flat?"

"I don't like big concrete structures. You never know if you'll walk out of them alive. John Edward went in for day surgery at Royal Prince Alfred and never came out again. I'll keep my feet firmly planted on the ground. High rises are death traps for elderly people like me."

Emily watched as Sylvia turned back to her stove. The enamel was chipped and worn but the surface was shiny clean. "Twelve minutes is all you need for scones. A minute more and they burn. Mother was always right in her baking advice."

"They look divine."

"It's the buttermilk. Makes them rise like topsy."

Sylvia turned stiffly. "If you would do the serving honours. I'm getting used to relying on you." She sat and Mimi sauntered over to her, whiskers tilted upwards to the delicious aroma.

Emily watched her tiny figure lean over to caress the dog. "She's aged recently," she mused, "and there's even less to her."

Emily sorted the tray and headed down the long hallway to the porch. Stained glass panels on either side of the front door threw warm red, green colours on the floorboards. Behind her, she heard Sylvia's soft footsteps.

"Slow down, Mimi, you'll be the death of me one day."

Mimi shot ahead and nuzzled Emily as she negotiated both the tray and the front screen door.

"If you're finished playing superwoman, I think I can manage opening the door for you." Sylvia planted her foot firmly on Emily's foot.

"Ouch."

"If that's what it takes to teach you to slow down."

Sylvia opened the screen door. "Look at this glorious afternoon. Golden sunshine straight from the heavens."

"I'm in too much pain to see it at the moment."

Sylvia laughed. "Serves you right."

A fresh posy of flowers stood in the jug. "I miss having a garden." Emily said. "There's something about being outdoors that's good for the soul."

"Are you a Christian woman?"

"I lost my faith years ago."

"I saw lots of that after the war. Can't say I blamed the boys, they saw shocking things over there."

She lifted the biscuit plate over. "Take a scone. There's cream and jam."

"I'm sorry, I can't. I'm watching my weight."

Sylvia's keen eyes fixed on her. "Why on earth are you watching your weight now? I'd understand if you were a young thing, looking for a nice fella. But you're done with that stage of your life, you can relax and eat some cream, surely?"

"I've been on a diet for thirty years, I don't have your thin shape. Menopause has hit my body hard and if I don't watch it, I'll look like a walking bowling ball."

"Suit yourself." Sylvia dabbed an enormous scoop of cream on her scone. "Mmm, it's amazing how good flour, milk and sugar are together." She looked up "There's Anzac biscuits too."

Emily shook her head.

"We baked so many batches to send overseas in the war. My fella loved them."

"They must've been pretty stale by the time they arrived overseas."

"Dunk them in tea and you'd never notice. John Edward said those biscuits reminded him of what he was fighting for."

At their feet, a riotous collection of Autumn flowers grew in the pot plants. Not a millimetre of soil was bare, leaves spilled onto the porch and trailed over the tiles.

"Who looks after your garden?"

"Our neighbour's boy does my lawn, has done so for the last 40 years. I look after the plantings on the porch, I love a colourful mass of flowers. John Edward said I was a generous gardener, never said no to a seedling. I was no Edna Walling."

"What was it like when you first bought in Erskineville?"

Sylvia dropped 3 slices of lemon and 2 teaspoons of sugar in her tea. "Very unlike today. We bought in '49 and it was a working class area. We couldn't afford a terrace and mother so wanted me to have the bedrooms upstairs. She said it was so refined to have your living and sleeping quarters separate. But our budget didn't stretch that far. As it turned out, we didn't need a lot of space so we stayed on. We'd catch a red rattler into the city on a Saturday night and meet friends for dinner on a Saturday night. Then we'd dance at a club, they had all the latest American tunes. It was glorious. We felt so lucky after the war, we could start again, put it behind us."

She shook her head and stared out at her garden. "It was harder for some of the boys, they never came right again. The weaker ones couldn't put it out of their minds, the killing and all. John Edward said it was biblically right to protect your homeland and if God was square with it, so was he."

"How did you meet?"

"He saw me out walking with friends at Adaminaby. We'd taken a long trail in the bush and were just coming out into a clearing. He christened me Sylvan Sylvie on the spot, said I was a wood nymph or some such nonsense. I never knew when he was joking or being serious."

Emily saw Sylvia's lip quiver as she hurriedly sipped some tea. Mimi nuzzled the aged lap and received a scone for her thoughtfulness. The drooling jaws demolished the treat and she lay her head in her lap again. Sylvia broke up another scone.

"I think dog biscuits would be better for her."

"Perhaps."

Emily shifted in her seat. "You must've missed the country when you left."

"Well, we never knew it would be permanent. John Edward always said we'd retire on the land. I was keen too, as I still had the family farm. We wanted acreage, to keep a few cattle and dogs. But when I lost him, the desire to move left me. I didn't want to leave the home I'd made with him. Too many memories and friends. Better to stay here than go back alone."

"It must be nice to have long term friends."

"You and your ex didn't?"

"We had lots of acquaintances. I dropped off their radar once the divorce was final. A book keeper isn't a social magnet in the circle we moved in. I was an outcast."

"I felt the same when I lost John Edward. A middle aged widow, without children, is an outcast in a different way." She ruffled Mimi's soft ears. "I mostly stayed in touch by phone from then onwards, it was easier."

"I can take you to see some of them if they're close by."

"No, thank you, the phone is enough."

"I'm sorry, I hope I haven't offended you.."

"There you go again, apologising. It's a bad habit, makes you sound nervous. Are you going to apologise for my growing old? I'm happy on my own, I don't need to be chauffeured around."

Sylvia stood and slowly straightened her back. "It's impossible to get comfortable in a wicker chair." She walked over to the railing and Mimi followed her.

"It's my turn to apologise to you. I was rude just then. But you get on my nerves with your apologies."

Emily went to speak but stopped.

"You were about to apologise again. I'll cure you of this habit in no time."

"You sound like a school teacher."

"Just what you need. And some cream and jam on your scones."

Emily stacked the tray. "I'll take these in."

Sylvia watched her in silence.

Emily entered the hallway and pushed Mimi away. "Go back to that bossy, old bird." She muttered.

She entered the kitchen and left the tray on the kitchen sink. "I feel like tipping it over the old shrew's head."

She stared at the tray and pots stacked in the sink. "I can't leave this for her," she thought, "She'll be tired after preparing it."

Emily washed and rinsed quickly.

"That's a long time to set a tray down on the bench." Sylvia stared at her from the doorway. "What are you doing, my girl? You're my guest."

"I'm sorry, I thought you'd be tired."

"There's that word again. Don't pity me, I manage very well. I know I speak plainly but I call it as I see it. Next time you visit, you must tell me about your life. I like to fill in the blanks."

Emily moved to the doorway. "Of course. Bye, Sylvia."

"Don't forget to walk Mimi later. She's made a perfect pig of herself just now. We need to walk off those scones."

Emily paused at the porch and stared at the flowers. She had a burning desire to pull them all out and leave them in a pile at the door. "Wouldn't that be good stress relief?" she mused.

Chapter 10

"Could my life get any more ridiculous?"

"Emms, you're hysterical. Start from the beginning. What's this about your neighbour's dog ruining your life?"

"Sue, I'm going on a date!"

Silence on the phone.

"Are you there?"

"With a man?"

"Oh God! I thought you knew I didn't bat for the other team."

Silence again.

"Does Bob want a second chance?"

"Do you think he's the only man I know?"

"I know he is."

"Well, I have workmates. Very attractive ones."

"You said you work with febrile dweebs."

Emily sighed. "This conversation is singularly unhelpful."

"Emms, I'm not used to you dating. Who?"

"Someone I met in the dog park."

"What! You don't meet men in parks. Just mums with prams and bloody exercise wankers. He wasn't wearing lycra, was he?"

"No, just walking his dog."

"You mean all I had to do to meet a bloke was buy a mutt?"

"Sue, I'm serious. What do I do? I can't go on a date, I haven't been on one for nearly thirty years."

"Same deal. You make small talk, praying they don't make even smaller talk. If they do, you make sure you order the most expensive meal and dessert. Might as well get full value for a boring night. What's his name?"

"Stan."

"Unfortunate. And surname?"

"No idea."

"That's unusual, granted. What's he look like?"

"A man."

"Tall or short?"

"Middle height."

"Fat or lean?"

"Middling."

"I can picture him now. When and where does the momentous date take place?"

"Oh God, tomorrow morning. We're going for coffee after dog walking."

"That's hardly a date!"

"It is for me. He suggested it and what could I say? No?"

"Hell no, that would be assertive."

"I'm sorry I called. What should I wear?"

"Clothes. It's like riding a bike, Emms."

Emily heard the shuffle of paper over the line.

"Let me know how you go. Good luck. Bye."

Emily stared at her computer screen as she hung up the phone.

"Here's your MYOB summary, I got it from the printer."

Emily started. "Oh thanks, Serena." She stared at her young workmate and not for the first time marvelled at how inappropriate her name was. Blond, corkscrew curls billowed over her shoulders Her small, thin frame was tightly trussed and she tottered on enormous heels. Red lips and lined eyes completed the picture.

"Much more Lolita." she pondered.

"How's Dominic? He's so sweet."

"Behind that sweet demeanour is a solid gold pig. I'd forgotten the meaning of sloth until he moved in."

"How can you say that about your own son?"

"Because it's true."

"Girls love him. Pity he's taken."

"Not now."

"Broken up with his girlfriend?"

Emily nodded.

"He won't be single long."

"You give me reason to live."

Serena sat on the edge of her desk. "You should invite him to the movies with us tonight. The whole office is going."

"No, tonight's clean up the mess in the spare bedroom night. Here's a question for you. What would you wear on a casual date?"

Serena laughed. "I don't do casual. But for your age bracket, it's probably best."

Emily had a sudden desire to staple her mouth shut.

"Wear something brighter and tighter. Your butt's still good, might as well show it off. Make sure you don't drink too much coffee or you'll go hyper and talk too much. I've heard you do it here."

Emily squeezed the stapler in her hands, to avoid temptation.

Serena stood. "Good luck on your date. Tell Dominic I said hi."

"Like hell I will." Emily thought, as she watched her totter away.

Chapter 11- View 1

"So she's not your dog?"

"I'm what's fashionably known as a dog walker. Unpaid but appreciated by her elderly owner."

Stan leaned back and winced. "These chairs guarantee quick customer turn around. No lingering with this murderous metal on your back."

Emily stroked Mimi, mostly to hide her shaking hands.

The waiter appeared with their coffees and Emily split her muffin in half and dropped it on the floor. Mimi devoured it immediately.

"She's on a special diet?"

"Her owner swears by croissants and muffins."

"My wife used to feed Ralf lasagne. Said it was good for his digestion."

"He's still here, so she wasn't wrong."

Stan bent to pat Ralf and Emily stared at him furtively. "I'm really getting on if I'm having coffee with such an old geezer," she mused. "Thinning, white hair, solid shape. Bob would love to see me come to this."

"Penny for your thoughts."

She choked on her latte. "I was checking out Ralf's fat ratio to Mimi's. She wins, paws down."

"My wife's not here any more to indulge him."

"I'm sorry."

"We planned to become grey nomads and travel Australia when I retired. The kids had moved out and I got a decent payout with Energy Australia. Then I lost her." He leaned back. "Bring my own chair next time."

Emily laughed.

"How are you so attractive and single?"

"My ex found someone younger and more attractive."

"How long were you together?"

"Twenty eight years."

"It's not easy, is it? My kids tell me to go out with my mates. But my mates still have their wives, so I don't ask them. If I'm invited for dinner, I feel like a third leg. What a whinge I'm having, you won't have coffee with me again."

"No, it's good to hear what it's like for a bloke. I'm new to it still, I can't even commit to hanging pictures in my flat. My kids don't get it, but they don't have thirty years of extra living up their sleeves. They look at everything with fresh eyes, which I love but it can drive me bonkers." She laughed. "See, it's my turn to whinge."

Stan nodded. "They'll turn us out of the cafe for gross morbidity. Which is marginally better than morbid obesity."

"You like word plays?"

"Love them. My wife and I played them all the time. She was sharper than me at it. We would do the Herald crossword together over breakfast. Do you like crosswords?"

"Hate them. I crochet."

He laughed.

"It's my only contact sport, just me and the needles." She shifted. "My routine is shot at the moment, my son has moved back temporarily. At least I hope it's temporary, he seems too comfortable!"

"It's nice to have the company, though. I have a granddaughter who's perfectly charming. I love her visiting, more so than her mother."

"Relationship a bit fraught between you?"

He nodded.

"I have the same issue with my daughter. What star sign is yours?"

"I don't follow the stars."

"What month was she born in then? I'll tell you."

"I don't believe in them. I'm a practising Christian. Salvo church."

Emily flushed. "Stan the Salvationist," she thought, "what do I say now?"

He leaned forward. "Don't worry, I take it as it comes but I say what I believe to be true."

"That's refreshing. A lot of people don't."

"You have any spiritual leanings?"

"As a kid, yes." Emily tossed the other half of the muffin to Mimi and watched her hoover the treat instantly. "But I lost it in my teenage years."

He looked at her inquisitively, a small smile on his lips.

"Difficult times and an indifferent family priest. He wouldn't help my mother at a time when we really needed the church's support. I decided then that God was a cold hearted bastard and his church reflected that. I stopped going after that."

"I hated him too, as a teenager. I ran from the truth, I felt safe in the arms of the wild world. We church people are responsible for driving away many good people with our words. I know my daughter feels the same way. Somehow the message got damaged in the delivery."

Emily made no reply.

She glanced at the other tables. Office workers relished the sunshine as they sat at the outdoor tables, laptops and mobile phones sprawled around them. Two grey haired, elegant women sat together, their gold jewellery reflecting in the sunshine. Emily touched her bare ring finger and wondered at its naked appearance.

He noticed the gesture. "You're not used to it."

"I don't think I ever will be. When I wore it, I was part of a tribe; married mothers, raising children ready to take over the world." She continued. "And they grew up, found their own place in the world and I lost mine somehow in the transition. I need another cappuccino."

"Me too."

Emily watched as he headed to the counter.

"Sue would approve," she thought, "he's paying."

As she waited, a late model BMW stopped at the pedestrian crossing alongside her table. A young woman sat at the wheel, turning to a crying toddler in the back seat. She gave a toy to the child and it held its hand out to receive it.

"Me, twenty years ago." Emily mused. "In my BMW with my babies." She watched as the car drove away.

Stan rejoined her. "I don't usually drink two coffees a day."

"I usually drink more."

Mimi whined. "Not too much longer, sweetie. I know you miss her."

"Is her owner nearby?"

"Next door to me. A plain speaking country woman of the war generation. Her stories and relish for life leave me feeling I missed something."

"I know what you mean. My parents were of that generation. My dad was a serving pastor in Papua New Guinea. He married my mum when he returned from overseas. He was forty eight and she was twenty five. It was quite a scandal in our church but she adored him. They lived for each other. I was blessed to grow up with that great love."

Emily shook her head. "I can't imagine what that would be like." She continued. "I don't mean to sound patronising but I admire the contribution the Salvos make. I always wanted to say that to an officer on collection day but felt like a wanker. Does that sound pretentious?"

"No."

"What do you do for the church, what's your field of volunteering?"

"None at the moment." Stan was silent as he stirred his coffee. "I've lied to you today. By omission."

Emily watched as he spoke quietly.

"I said to you I say what I believe to be true." He leaned forward. "My wife's not dead. She's in a nursing home with Alzheimer's disease. I placed her in care a year ago, just for a break-I was exhausted."

Emily didn't interrupt.

"I visit her every day, after I walk Ralf. In the beginning, she brightened up at the sight of me and I thought good care would improve her condition. But institutionalised care is what it is and now she's deteriorated to the point where she doesn't recognise me.

And I can't take her back because I can't be her husband and her nurse."

Emily reached over and squeezed his hand. "I'm sorry, Stan." He looked away. "I knew you'd be lovely about it. You have such kind eyes. I meant to tell you straight away but it was so nice to talk to a woman, not explain my situation as if it were the summary of my life." He stood.

"You don't need to go."

"Thanks, but I need to get to the nursing home by morning tea. Alice can be restless in the afternoon. I feel better when we have a good visit together."

"I hope we have coffee again. I'd like to hear more about her and your kids."

He seemed to almost bow to her, then gathered his leash and moved away silently.

Emily stirred the remains of her latte. "C'mon, Mims, let's get you home."

A short time later, she stood in her kitchen, looking out at the streetscape below. In the distance, she heard Mimi bark. Emily twirled the chalk between her fingers as she stared at the board. She lifted her hand and wrote:

"A lovely man loses his wife and I gain a friend and a new view of me: kind eyes."

Chapter 12 - Round 1

"Hi, I'm Emily." She sat beside the petite, blonde woman. "Do you mind if I sit here? I live in apartment number seven."

"I looked at that one! Too small for me, I wanted three bedrooms." The woman turned to speak to someone on her left.

Emily glanced at the blonde's heavily lacquered hair. A strong perfume hit her nostrils.

A small group of people sat on the outdoor retaining wall.

"Gus, I think everyone that's coming is here now, why don't you start the meeting?" The unnamed woman beside Emily called out. "As Chairperson, it's your duty to start on time. We all have commitments."

"Not yet, Cecilia. Rhonda's running a bit late." He rustled the notes in his hand and looked away.

The woman beside Emily sighed. "Pompous git," she murmured, "he'll drag this out until his partner in crime gets here."

Behind her, the sound of someone running down the stairs of the complex and the front security door was flung open. "Sorry I'm late, all! Thanks for waiting for me."

"We had no choice," murmured the petite one.

"Rhonda, we wouldn't start without you." Gus waited until she was seated, then opened his colour coded notes.

The latecomer sat on the other side of Emily, her enormous frame filling the hollows of Emily's slender body.

"You're new here," she whispered loudly. "I've seen you walking a dog some mornings."

"It's my neighbour's."

"You don't mean the old woman who lives next door?"

"Yes, Sylvia."

"Is she family?" Rhonda pursed her lips and Emily watched the effect it had on her appearance. "Note to self; pursed lips are not a good look for middle aged woman," she mused.

"No, we met by chance." Emily responded. "She's a real character."

"Isn't she an absolute cow!" Rhonda leaned closer. "We've had no end of trouble with her. We've asked for a 10pm curfew with her music at night. That bloody opera goes on past midnight some nights."

Emily nodded. "Well, it's her home. She's been here a lot longer than this complex."

"Times change. It's communal living now. I don't know if you've noticed but the sound insulation in this building is appalling, noise goes right through the walls. We've tried to make her understand but she tells us to go away. She threatened to turn her dog on me once, then she said I should get a dog, judging by the size of me. Offensive old bitch."

Emily felt a sharp pain in her side as Rhonda's weight compressed her hip.

"You could be our emissary. Perhaps she'd listen to you."

"I've only known her a month."

"Well, if she hasn't told you to bugger off yet, you're one up on us." Rhonda called out "Gus, I think we have a negotiator between us and the old lady next door." She pointed to Emily, who prayed she wouldn't lean any closer.

Gus lifted his head from his notes and stared. His lips pursed like Rhonda's and Emily shuddered to herself.

"Really?" he spoke quietly as he crossed over to Emily. "I can't sleep," he leaned over her, "some nights she turns her music up to torment me." He bent over Emily, who had the uncomfortable sensation she was about to receive a benediction. "If you could help, that would be lifesaving."

She shifted backwards to distance herself. "I'll think about it," she replied.

Gus dropped to his knees in front of her. "I've even thought of moving up the coast to get away from the noise."

Rhonda squeezed his arm. "Don't you do that to me, Gus. You can't leave me here with her!" She threw a glance at the coiffured woman on the other side of Emily.

"Gus, I insist we start the meeting now." Cecilia raised her hand. "People have families to go home to. Maybe you and Rhonda can spend all afternoon chatting but Stephen and I are out to dinner with friends tonight."

"I'm introducing myself to our new neighbour." He stood stiffly and opened his notes.

"Welcome everyone. Sorry we're holding the annual committee meeting later than usual, but we held off for Cecilia to return from overseas. Really, I think next time you should give a proxy vote to one of us."

She didn't reply but looked down at her meeting notes.

Emily watched the proceedings. The group were all middle aged, except for an elderly man and woman who sat in fold up chairs. The old woman knitted as she listened, her head tilted to catch the dialogue. Her ball of wool twirled around her chair and the man bent continuously to untangle it.

Emily smiled down at her. "I love to crochet."

The old woman stared at her.

"She must be deaf." Emily thought.

"Last bloody time I attend one of these," Emily pondered, "beyond boring." She lifted her face to the sun as Gus ran through the audit and expenses for the year.

"We can read these figures in our summaries." Cecilia interrupted him. "I notice there's eleven of us here, which is good for casting a vote. Why don't we skip to Motion 3. Everyone agree?"

Gus stopped speaking.

He and Rhonda pursed their lips in unison.

"Tension in the air," Emily thought as she sat upright, "this could get interesting."

"Cecilia, we've spoken to you before about interrupting proceedings."

"Gussy, that's well and good but I have an early dinner date and I really want to hear this motion." Cecilia's faded blue eyes widened at him.

Emily saw a pulse beat in his red neck.

"You can do the rest afterwards. We can be flexible in these meetings. Please, fussy Gussy."

Emily thought the vein would pop in his neck. His lips tightened to the thinnest of slivers.

"Go on mate, she's right. We can all read." A tall man chimed in.

"What apartment are you in?"

"I'm not, mate, I own number 19 as an investment property. Let's go to Motion 3."

An approving murmur went around the crowd.

Gus and Rhonda glanced at each other.

"OK," Gus spoke, "if you're happy to skip the financials, we'll take a motion later approving the figures. Better hope we're not cooking the books."

Rhonda joined in. "It won't be our fault if things go pear shaped around here."

"Like your butt." Emily caught Cecilia's whispered words.

"Motion 3," Gus read from his summary and Emily noticed his hands were shaking. "It is proposed by Unit 15 to place a fountain in the centre of the front lawn, to be connected to the water tank. The fountain would run entirely on tank water, with no detriment to our water usage."

Rhonda stood. "What a ridiculous proposal! It'll look dreadful in that small patch of lawn and we'll have to rip up the grass to lay the pipes and plumbing. An absolute waste of money."

Cecilia smiled, exposing capped, white teeth. "We already have the pipes laid out from the sprinkler system." She stood and faced the crowd. "It's a small, very elegant fountain, a really lovely statement piece." She reached down to a cloth bag at her feet. "I bought this in Italy last year and wanted to place it on my terrace but it was too impractical with the drainage. Rather than put it into storage, I'm happy to share it with the complex. It will look perfectly lovely in the grounds and we need a piece to anchor the greenery."

Rhonda rolled her eyes as Cecilia lifted a stone statue of a boy from the bag. Parts of the stone were blackened and a small chip indented its chubby shoulder.

"That's sweet!" Emily exclaimed.

Gus and Rhonda glared at her and she shrank back.

"We have a native garden," Gus stared at the cherub, "it will look inappropriate, too ethnic."

"Absolutely," Rhonda followed on, "look at it, it's mouldy and broken. They saw you coming, Cecilia."

"It's an antique," Cecilia stared at Rhonda. "It's meant to have flaws. Not everyone loves reproductions."

Rhonda's face reddened.

Gus bent down to the statue. "Where does the water spout from?" He squinted at the cherub. "Oh, surely not! From his little willy."

"Oh, that's classic!" Rhonda clapped her hands.

"It's quirky, I admit it." Cecilia held the statue up. "But it's gorgeous when set up. We need to add some personal touches to the garden, it's way too Spartan as is."

"I think so too..." Emily hesitated as Gus and Rhonda glared at her again.

"Why don't we trial it for a year?" Cecilia smiled at the crowd.

"I like it," the tall man spoke up. "I saw tons of those fountains in Spain last year."

The old lady looked up from her knitting. "I like it, Cecilia, the water will be soothing. Maybe we could place a seat behind it and I could knit there in the afternoon. I could pretend I was in Italy."

Her husband nudged her. "Flossie, if that transports you to Italy so easily, I'd have bought you a statue years ago. Saved myself a fortune."

Gus interrupted. "Think seriously about this. If it looks daft, we'll have to replace the lawn. It all costs money."

"Gussy," Cecilia spoke. "This is our home and we need to make it as lovely as we can. If everyone's agreeable, we can install it next month. The lawn will bounce back, grass always grows back. Just like hair." She looked at his thinning pate. "Well, not always."

Emily watched the nerve pulse in his throat.

"I'm against it." Rhonda spoke. "A complete waste of money."

"Let's vote." Gus eyed the crowd. "All those in favour of trialling the fountain, raise your hands."

Emily watched as five hands rose in the air. She sat on hers and noted the wistful expression on Cecilia's face.

"What are you doing?" Rhonda whispered to her. "Don't raise your hand, she'll get her way."

"But it's so good of her to share it with us."

"You bloody idiot!"

Cecilia clapped her hands. "That's great, we got the majority vote! Thank you, everyone." She smiled at Emily. "You should join our committee this year. Fresh faces are always good."

"Oh, no, no. I have too many commitments as it is..."

"Nonsense, always ask a busy person to do things, that way the job gets done. Please."

Emily gulped at the beaming smile Cecilia threw her way.

"OK, just for this year." She saw Gus and Rhonda glance at each other and she spoke.

"That's so good." Cecilia hugged her. "We're a friendly mob, aren't we, Gussy?"

He didn't reply as he shuffled his colour coded notes.

"I'm a bloody idiot" Emily thought, "I walk the dog of an autocratic old woman and now I'm entangled in a committee of silent assassins. I have no backbone. I deserve this."

Chapter 13

"Matt, how good to see you. Sarah likes to hide you from us."

"It's true, she wants to keep me pure."

"Hey, Snow White." Dominic held his hand out. "It's probably me that she's protecting you from. I'm the mad one."

"Right again." Matt grinned as he shook hands.

"Where is she?" Emily peered outside her door.

"Trying to find a park outside, swearing her head off. Guest parking was full."

"And she didn't let you do it? Let me guess, she'd do a better job."

"Yeah." Matt grinned at Dominic. "Got any beer?"

"First thing I stacked in Mum's fridge."

"And only thing," Emily called out from the kitchen. "Leave the door ajar, boys. And maybe leave lollies on the hall stand to sweeten Sarah's mood. It worked when she was little."

"Might take more than that tonight." Matt murmured.

"Oh dear." Emily stirred her casserole. "We're in for it."

"Not me." Dominic jumped up from the sofa. "I'll head out to the movies."

"No, you won't." She waved her ladle at him. "I've invited both my kids for dinner. We've got to make time for each other now."

"Mum, I live here. You see me all the time."

"No, just your breakfast plate in the sink and pyjamas on the bathroom floor of a morning. Which you need to pick up. Seriously."

"Why are you going into the en-suite anyway?"

"Toilet roll and soap checks. Old habits die hard."

"Obviously. Oh, I forgot the beer! Sorry, Matt."

"Bloody Erskineville! Absolutely no parking." They all turned as Sarah walked into the room. "Mum, you should've got a two car garage."

"My budget didn't stretch that far." Emily walked across to kiss her.

"How are you, darling?"

"Ravenous. Oh God, is that your chicken casserole I can smell? It is! I haven't had that in ages. Matt, this is Mum's best dish." Sarah leaned over the stove. "Hey, Dom." She turned to acknowledge him. "Guzzling free beer, huh?"

"No, getting one for your paramour. He needs a drink, you obviously drive men to it."

"Ha, ha." She sipped some sauce from the casserole. "Try this, Matt. I can never make it like this."

"It's the bay leaves." Emily spoke. "Keep stirring, honey. I can rest my legs, I haven't stopped today."

"Do you have any white wine, Mum? This needs a drop."

"I don't use wine in casseroles."

"The French use it in everything. Remember in Marseilles, Matt, the chef in that small restaurant? He doused everything in wine."

"Ah, the French!" Dominic sat alongside Emily. "Marinated casseroles one day, marinated cornflakes the next. Kids must be positive piss heads."

"You're so crass." Sarah looked at him.

"And you're so pretentious."

"I don't know how French birds stay so skinny," Matt spoke up, "I put on weight over there."

"Portion control." Sarah waved the ladle. "They only eat enough to stay thin and nervous. As Kate Moss says, nothing tastes as good as skinny feels."

"A philosopher." Dominic drained his beer. "Another one, Matt?"

Matt glanced at Sarah and she nodded. "I'll drive."

She tested the sauce again. "This is done."

Emily stood. "I'll serve, you all sit."

She watched the boys cross the room, equals in height and languid motion. Sarah followed behind them, a frown between her blue eyes as she read her phone messages.

Emily placed the casserole dish on the table and raised her glass. "Our first meal here together, cheers everyone."

"Cheers, Mum."

"That looks delicious."

Sarah looked up. "Dad's taking Elspeth to France for the European summer. He's hoping she'll do a cooking course he's booked for her in Provence. Remember he used to say he'd send you there when we were kids? I guess you were too good a cook and didn't need the classes."

Emily concentrated on her cutlery as she spoke. "When do they go?"

"June, for six weeks. Elspeth's a darling but she can't cook to save herself. Too much brown rice and broccoli for my taste. Give me a casserole any day."

"Indeed," Emily twirled her wine glass. "The GFC mustn't be biting advertising agencies too hard."

"Oh no, he's won some big account in Melbourne and got a huge bonus. He and Elspeth closed the deal over dinner at some hotel. Apparently she clicked with the wife of the advertising head."

Emily watched as Sarah poured herself a glass of red wine. She lifted an eyebrow at her but Sarah shrugged and turned to murmur something to Matt.

Dominic bent towards her. "Dad wasn't keen on you finding out about the holiday. He thinks you're still bitter about losing the house."

"I see." She drained her glass and re-filled it immediately. She held the crystal glass in her hand. It was a wedding gift and one of the few things she took from the old home. She held it aloft to the light and watched as rainbow colours lit the patterned crystal. "I loved this set of glasses as soon as I saw them," she spoke, "I thought they were the start of a new and better life."

Dominic squeezed her hand. "I'm glad you kept them. Elspeth would serve some disgusting health concoction in them."

She turned to Matt. "Help yourself, honey." She watched as he scooped another ladle onto his plate.

His gentle features caught at her heart. "Antithesis of Sarah," she reflected, "sweet and calm. Needs direction and she has that in spades."

She watched as Sarah finished her small portion of casserole and scoop a serve of salad onto her plate. "My careful girl," she thought, "always prudent. Apple didn't fall far from the tree."

She lifted her fork and swallowed a mouthful. "Provence." The word sat on her tongue, poisoning her taste buds. "A long promised treat for a long suffering wife." She mused. "What a fool I was. What a fool I am, dog walking and having coffee with lost men."

"Emily."

She looked up.

"I've been promoted to a Vice Principal position. I start officially in three months."

"Matt, I'm delighted for you! Sarah, you didn't say a word."

"We didn't want to say anything until we knew."

"A high school, Matt?"

He nodded. "The principal, Mr Campbell, is brilliant. All about nurturing teachers and students to excel. We got on so well in the interview, I had three all up. He's going to be a brilliant mentor, I know it."

"Well deserved. Where's the school?"

"Central Coast, Gosford High. It's a selective school."

"That's a long commute from Sydney! I know people do it but it must be draining."

Matt glanced at Sarah before he replied.

She nodded.

"We thought we'd try living on the Central Coast to see if we like it. We know a few people up there already and we can afford to buy a house. With Sydney prices, we'll never be able to live near the sea and I'd miss my surfing."

"Cool move, bro." Dominic nodded. "You'll be completely isolated, with Sarah in control. You'll never see the ocean again, just the inside of an IKEA Supercenta. How I envy you."

Matt laughed. "Piss off, you bastard. She's not as tough as you think."

"Watch and learn."

Sarah leaned forward. "I've been checking the internet, Mum. We can buy a three bedroom house in Gosford for the same price as a two bedroom flat in the inner west. We can use Matt's inheritance from his grandmother as our deposit. It just makes sense."

Dominic leaned back in his chair. "You'll be surrounded by bogans. What'll you do for work?"

"There's heaps of casual teaching work up there. Matt has to establish his career first, then I can step up." She turned towards Emily. "What do you think?"

"I think you're both incredibly smart and focused. I could barely tie my laces together at your age."

She raised her glass. "To both of you, all the luck in the world."

Sarah clinked glasses. "It's ok, I can drink, Mum."

Emily refilled her own glass again. "I'll pay for this tomorrow," she thought, "but it's getting me through tonight."

"Relax, kids, I'll stack the dishwasher. Dom, break out the cheese platter."

…......................

Sarah rubbed Matt's back as they lay on the sofa.

"Do you miss Jenny?"

Dominic looked up from the armchair nearby. "Why do you ask?"

"I'm curious. I couldn't imagine not having Matt, we've been through so much together. Teaching college, the oldies' divorce. It'd be like severing an artery."

He was silent.

Emily interrupted from the kitchen. "I'm sure it's hard for him."

"I didn't ask you. Well?"

Dominic shrugged. "It's different for everyone. We weren't like you and Matt, we made no plans for a future together. Just drifted along, until one day we drifted apart."

"I wonder if Jenny would describe it in the same way."

"She's a girl, of course she wouldn't."

"I miss her, she was fun to be around." Sarah glanced at Dominic. "And she was good for you."

"Obviously."

"You should ask her to come back."

"Obviously not. She wanted something I wasn't."

"That's sad." Sarah squeezed his arm.

Dominic was silent again.

Emily watched him. His dark curls fell on his forehead, the way they did when he was a toddler. She lifted a hand instinctively to caress them. Somehow, somewhere, he was still her small, perfect child.

Chapter 14

"You're my Dutch courage."

"Why's that?" Sylvia looked over her teacup at Emily.

"I'm visiting a girlfriend in hospital this week. She's having a hysterectomy for cervical cancer."

"Poor thing. Send her my best wishes."

"I will. Thanks."

Sylvia stared out at her garden. The lawn was overgrown from recent rain and a profusion of weeds spiked through the soil.

"You look a bit tired today, my girl."

"I am a bit. I've worked overtime this week."

"I was speaking to Mimi but the same could be said of you."

Emily laughed. "Must learn my place." She sat back in her chair. "That's a lesson we learn at mama's knee."

"You know I'm grateful for your help."

"I do, Sylvia. And I did go on a muffin date with Mimi."

"Who was the gentleman?"

"A fellow dog owner."

"You must tell me when the next date is. I'll spruce Mimi up."

Emily was silent.

"She didn't disgrace herself and eat his muffin too?"

"No, she was a lady to the end. Stan and I say hello at the park, but there's nothing to it."

"Shame, you're still young enough to start again with someone. You're a born carer." She leaned back in her chair. "I was set in my ways when I lost John Edward, I had no desire to marry again."

"I know how you feel. My ex, Bob, went from me to his current wife. I wouldn't dream of doing that."

"I know how you feel. When I first lost John Edward, I thought my heart would stop beating."

"Really?"

"I stood beside his hospital bed and prayed I would die too. I knew I would never accept his loss." She continued. "I remember the next morning so clearly. John Edward's glasses were on the side table, folded up on the book he was reading. I rolled over to say good morning to him and remembered he wasn't there. In that second, I realised I would just mark time."

"Did you work, Sylvia?"

"No, my girl. In my day, we let our men support us and we created a wonderful home life for them. Seems to me that wasn't a bad model for Australian society to aspire to. If women were home, there would be so many more jobs for poor, unemployed men today."

"Lucky you're saying this in the privacy of your own home. Any women under 60 would shoot you for such treacherous words."

"I'd say it aloud today. It's a free country. In his heyday, I rang John Laws and aired my views quite a few times. He was such a dear man, so respectful and polite. His Caroline never worked a day in her life."

"On his salary, she could have paid someone to breathe for her." Emily remarked. "Life's so expensive today and mortgages are astronomical. Women need to be in the workforce and they need fulfilling careers."

"Poppycock. We've raised a generation of latchkey children and homes bereft of motherly care. In my day, a woman was a helpmate, not an income earner. Families are falling apart and people are drifting into relationships built on shifting sand." Sylvia raised the teapot. "Another cuppa?"

"Please."

Emily watched her lift the pot, and pour the tea unsteadily.

"What was Adaminaby like when you were a child?"

"You're changing the subject. I can see you don't approve of my views."

"I find them charming but antiquated."

"Hmmph."

"And Adaminaby?"

Sylvia laughed. "I'll tell you because you're gracious. Not all women are. Can't tell you how many people I've offended in the past by being forthright. I was raised to speak plainly and I can't change now."

"Your folks were country people, I assume."

"From generations back. Farm passed down from my great grandfather. My nephew has the sheep station now, all modern and cost effective. I remember the shearers of my childhood; gallant, skilled men. Mother was forever cooking giant pot roasts and lamb stews. Have you ever smelled scones cooking in an Aga stove? That's something to experience."

"You must've been a big help to her."

"Good Lord, no!" Sylvia rocked with laughter. "I mustered with my father. He called me his second son, I was that good on a horse. I wanted to do eventing at shows but we didn't have the time or money to spare on such luxuries. I had a good seat, I was slight but steady on a horse."

"So you did men's work?"

Sylvia nodded.

"You've just gone against your argument of a woman's place being in the home."

"The farm was my home and we all had to muck in."

"Except in the kitchen."

"You're not much of a guest if you contradict me."

"Sorry, Sylvia, I'm giving you a hard time."

"You were doing so well until now! You didn't apologise once to me. I'll break you of this habit before I die."

"Old habits die hard."

She watched Sylvia break off a croissant for Mimi. "She's getting rounder every day."

"Life's too short not to eat pastries. Middle age is the time to reward yourself for surviving. Leave the diets for the pretty, young things looking for good husbands."

"I'll pretend I didn't hear that." Emily laughed. "And what about John Edward, were his family country folk too?"

"No," Sylvia shook her head. "His father was transferred from Sydney by the Education Department, to run the local primary school in town. They were considered quite sophisticated. My mum never felt comfortable around them, she wasn't a great reader and all they spoke of was books and ideas. I tried to read the books they recommended but it was all gibberish to me. D.H. Lawrence was a strange fella."

Emily laughed. "Yes, he was."

Sylvia continued. "John Edward loved poetry. He read the works of Keats, Shelley and Lord Byron. He had a beautiful, deep voice. I would close my eyes when he read to me, I couldn't believe such a wonderful man loved me. I was thrilled to be his girl."

Emily was silent as Sylvia spoke on.

"My family didn't have radio, not till after the war, so we made our own fun. He and I would walk through the fields with a picnic lunch and plan our lives together. He wanted to try the city, see if we could make some good money and buy land to retire to. He was ambitious and I knew I could adapt. So I saved a small dowry for myself, it came in handy when I arrived in Sydney. Then after the war, John Edward studied at university to get qualifications."

"Hard times?"

"No, thrilling. We were that keen to get ahead. I worked as a secretary to a Professor and Johnny stacked shelves at night to pay our board. We barely saw each other for three years but it was worth it."

Emily raised her eyebrows.

"What does that mean?"

"You worked!"

Sylvia laughed. "Jobs were plentiful back then. Not so many boys came back."

"You're a bundle of contradictions, Sylvia."

"Indeed I'm not. What a thing to say!"

Emily stood. "I should be heading off. Thanks for tea. I'll collect Mims late this afternoon." She walked into the strong sunlight and turned to wave.

Sylvia's gaze was dreamy. She huddled in her chair, looking at the floor, revisiting a vivid past.

Emily could visualise her running through fields, a slip of a girl with a handsome, dark haired boy beside her. The blue grey colours of the bush imprinting their love for eternity.

She turned abruptly and headed to her apartment. She passed the meticulous hedges and saw the gardener digging in the centre of the lawn. He pushed a straw hat back on his head as Gus pointed out the area to be cleared. Emily avoided his eye as she entered the block.

Chapter 15

"You did that as a little boy." Emily stepped out onto the balcony. "You'd hunch your shoulders and get a faraway look in your eyes, like an old man contemplating his past."

Dominic nodded. "I feel like an old man today."

She brushed the curls from his forehead. "Missing her?"

He nodded.

"I miss my old life too." Emily leaned over the railings. "The familiarity of it." She sighed. "Some mornings, I'm afraid to walk out the door. Isn't that silly?"

Dominic placed an arm over her shoulder. "You should've told Dad to piss off years ago. Us too."

The night air was scented. A flowering jasmine grew in a large terracotta pot on the balcony alongside. Its white flowers visible in the dark as a delicate perfume carried in the breeze. Night sounds. Pale, low stars in the clear sky.

Emily watched Dominic closely. His frame was thinned by a grief she was not privy to. The long lashes that swept over his eyes shielded any expression.

"You got your dad's good looks." She caressed his hair. "I've always been proud of my handsome son."

He was silent.

"Maybe all you need is some time away from each other."

"I'll never grow old with someone."

The words were spoken so low, she barely heard them.

"Don't say that Dom, you're just in a bad patch."

"It won't happen." He turned to her.

"It's within me, a certainty that I won't have that life. That I don't want that life."

She stared at him. "Is that what you told Jenny?"

"Yes."

"But why? You're young, educated, intelligent."

"Adjectives not indicative of my heart."

"And what is?"

"Detached. I observe people, I analyse their characters. When I understand them, I discard them."

"Did you do that to Jenny?"

"Yes."

"Poor girl."

He turned away and stared out at the street.

"Maybe you're afraid of pain, you watched our family disintegrate."

"No."

She stopped. The breeze picked up and she wrapped her cardigan closer. It seemed to separate them. Dominic felt aloof to her touch as she hugged him.

"I'm the King of futility. Jenny and I went to a wedding a few months ago. She was caught up in the manufactured romance of the day, the dresses, flowers and photography. I felt a hundred years old, I could see the bride and groom in five years time, hating each other and the smallness of their lives. I told Jenny as much and she was distraught." He ran his hand over the balcony rail. "I asked her to come to South America with me, see passionate people dancing on the edge of poverty. She looked like I had broken her favourite toy." He laughed. "That's when I knew we wouldn't make it."

"But you love her."

"But not what she wants from me. I have no intention of adding another wailing soul to this planet."

"Now, that would hurt a girl."

"And yet I love her, always will. I can't bend her to my world view but I can't forget her." He shrugged. "Now, there's a troubled image for you."

Emily leaned over the railing and looked down at the lawn. The newly installed fountain stood in the centre. The cherub's head was lit by down-lights in the garden beds. She peered closer. "What's that on the grass? I think it's an arm! The statue's been damaged."

She gasped. "Cecilia will have a pink fit."

"It that the skinny blonde who wears overpowering perfume?"

She nodded.

"I don't know how her husband holds down his food."

"You haven't smelt his aftershave." She peered closely at the statue. "At least his willy is still intact. That's the centrepiece, so to speak."

"Many a woman has said the same."

She laughed and squeezed his arm. "Don't give up on yourself. The boring dream of a house in the suburbs and kids may kick in for you one day."

"I don't think you've listened to me." Dominic looked down and held a finger to his lips. "Someone's down there." He pointed downwards and Emily saw a shadow pass on the far side of the lawn and disappear onto the street.

"Oh my God, Dom!" she whispered back. "They must have broken the arm off."

"Looks like we're not in Kansas anymore, Dorothy."

"People are bonkers here." Emily tugged his sleeve. "It's rather entertaining in a way."

"I'm heading to bed. Let me know if anything else gets chopped off." He bent over and kissed her. "Night, Mum."

She felt his dry kiss on her cheek. "Night, son."

She glanced across to Sylvia's home. The front lawn was in darkness but she thought she discerned Mimi sleeping on the front porch. She heard the soft strains of an aria.

"She really loved that man," she mused, "her one and only." She glanced back to the lounge room. "I wonder if Dom has thrown away his one and only." She rested her weight on the railing and breathed in the jasmine scent. "I wonder if we all have one defining love and some of us never meet them? We wander this world looking for something we can't define or explain."

The breeze lifted and she felt the rush of air on her skin. Like a long lost caress on her body.

Chapter 16

"How's the new boyfriend?"

Serena sat on a corner of the desk as Emily looked up.

"You went on a date last month, remember?"

"Oh, the coffee! It was pleasant, he's a nice man."

"God, is that the way old people describe dates?"

Emily glanced furtively at her stapler, as Serena twirled a corkscrew curl. "Dom OK? Over his ex now?"

"I think he'll always be sad about her."

"He'll hook up with someone new."

"He won't forget Jenny in a hurry."

An expression in the young woman's eyes that Emily couldn't read. "You say."

"I know my own son."

"So when do you see the old guy for coffee again?"

"That depends on our dogs."

Serena nodded. "Must be nice to meet in a park. I love quiet dates, walking on a beach or kissing under the stars. That's the best." Her hair fell forward, concealing her eyes. "I went on a date once with a guy who took me fishing. We sat in his dinghy all day and he taught me how to hook tackle and angle. Didn't try to kiss me once. I was so pissed off." She laughed. "Even when you get what you want, you don't want it."

"Profound, Serena." Emily bent down to her spreadsheet. "I'd better finish this."

Serena stood. "Say hi to Dom for me."

"I always do."

Chapter 17 - Round 2

"I'm shocked." Cecilia stared at the committee members. "That statue cost me two thousand euro and it's ruined."

"We can dismantle it on the weekend." Gus chimed in. "You can put it on your terrace. At least it'll be safe there."

"It'll look more authentic," Rhonda spoke, "all great statues are ruined. I thought when I was last in Europe that the lot of them needed a good scrub and a bit of super-glue."

Emily watched closely. "Are they winding her up?" she wondered. She looked at Rhonda's face as she spoke again.

"Must've been the neighbourhood kids. They probably thought it was a laugh. It's a shame."

Cecilia and Emily stared at her. "Just glue it back on."

Flossie knitted as she spoke. "I've a new granddaughter." She smiled at Emily. "Seems I'm forever knitting pink cardigans." She tapped her needle on Gus' arm. "Glue it back on."

"It's not a clean break." He pulled his arm away. "Three fingers broke off in the fall. The glue will look tacky and won't dry with the water. You'd need to stand by the fountain 24/7 with a tub of araldite to seal it down."

"Shut the fountain off for a week." Flossie tugged at the wool as she spoke. "Give it time to set. We can put a 'trespassers will be prosecuted' sign at the entrance, to scare the kids off. Or whoever it was."

"Flossie, what kind of philistine are you? We will not be super glueing the statue." Cecilia looked stern over her stylish glasses.

Emily stared as Cecilia's botoxed forehead attempted to frown. A faint upper wiggle, then complete stillness. A vein bulged in the centre and Emily stared as it seemed to enlarge with Cecilia's flushed countenance.

"I like to sit behind it." Flossie looked up from her needles. "I get an hour's worth of sun. The birds love it; sometime I bring seeds."

Rhonda pursued her lips. "You'll bring rats."

"She said seeds, not cheese." Cecilia interrupted. "We did say we'd trial the fountain for a year. Do I need to contact the other owners if you two insist on reneging on the agreement we made at the Annual Meeting? Or my solicitor?"

Gus and Rhonda were silent.

Cecilia gave a small smile. "I'll look up marble restorers in Sydney. I'll try to cap the expenses as best I can but I do want my statue repaired. It's only just."

"It won't hurt to try." Emily ventured. "I do like the sound of the fountain when I have coffee on my balcony of a morning."

They stared at her.

"It's soothing..." her voice trailed off.

"Try throwing seeds," encouraged Flossie, "you'll be amazed what turns up!"

"Oh shut up!" Rhonda spoke. "That wool is starting to muddle your brain." She rolled the committee notes in her hand. "If that's the only item on the agenda, I'll leave."

"Good idea," rejoined Gus, "the three of you are ganging up on us. If you all insist on resurrecting that thing, so be it." He glanced at Emily, who felt her stomach lurch.

She tried to smile as she spoke. "Well, lets …."

Gus and Rhonda turned as one and headed up the stairs.

"Cecilia," Flossie tapped her arm with her needles, "would you disentangle me?"

"Of course." Cecilia bent down and unwound the wool from the fold up chair. "Be careful, I might wrap you up like an Egyptian mummy."

"And I might tell everyone the fountain has bird lice."

They stared at each other. Then stood and walked in different directions.

Emily watched in silence, the only committee member left behind.

Chapter 18

Emily peered at the figure in the hospital bed. "Hey, Casper."
"White as, huh?" Sue lay still, her fingers twitching on the bed sheet.
Emily lay a bunch of flowers on the bedside table. "No doubt the nurses will provide vases for the vast array of flowers due to arrive shortly."
"Yeah, right. I've told no one I'm here. My staff think I'm on holiday."
"What, didn't play sympathy card? I'd have milked it dry." Emily automatically tucked the hospital blanket into the lightweight mattress.
Sue glanced down. "As long as I don't look like I'm in a shroud. Don't want to look like Lazarus in private cover." She yawned. "What time is it?"
"3.30." Emily sat beside the bed and motioned to the catheter in Sue's arm. "How do you feel?"
"Like a truck's run over my fanny."
"Ouch!" Emily gently touched her arm. "What did they yank out?"
"Bits and pieces I didn't need. Uterus and cervix."
"Complete hysterectomy, huh?"

Sue motioned to the water jug. "A glass, Emms." She stared down at the bed sheet. "I don't want to see the scar."
"It'll heal. You'll be back in bikinis in no time."
"Thanks, that was uppermost in my mind."
"I thought so."
The overhead TV switched on above the bed alongside Sue. They watched as a game show host ran past a floodlight path of lights and screaming contestants.
"Lord, give me strength." Sue whispered. "If she turns the volume up, I'll throw my drip stand at her."
"Suzie! Can you be held in custody after major surgery?"
"I hope I don't find out." Sue leaned back against her pillows and picked at the sheet with her nails.

"If you keep that up," Emily leaned over, "a vase might be flung back at you."

Emily looked about the room. A stark twin share room, with reproduction paintings and expensive equipment that beeped intermittently.

"When can you get up?"

"Not till tomorrow." Sue sighed. "I'm chained to this bed for another twelve hours. And then five days in hospital. Can you believe it?"

"Not everyone's a human dynamo. I'd quite like it myself, it's the only place the kids couldn't hound me and I'd be free of dog walking duties. Lucky you!"

Sue sighed again. "Can you hand me my mobile? It's inside the cabinet, tucked into my cream shirt pocket."

"What's so urgent?"

"Work, I like to read my emails."

"Aren't you on complete bed rest?"

Sue was silent.

"And what would that do to your blood pressure?"

"You aren't my mother."

"In this situation, I'm as good as." Emily sat, unmoving. "You can rip your stitches open tomorrow, hunting for your phone."

"Ew, Emms! Some friend you are."

"Life's a bitch."

"No, just you."

"Touche"'

"What time is it?"

"Are we there yet?" Emily mimicked. "It's ten minutes later than when you last asked." She looked up as the tea lady wheeled a trolley into the room. "How lovely, an afternoon cuppa."

"Would you like one, lovey?"

"Please." Emily smiled at the elderly woman. She touched Sue's arm. "What about you, Casper?"

Sue looked away.

Emily noticed the tea lady's lips purse as she left a teapot on the bedside tray. She left two cups and thrust a packet of biscuits into Emily's hand as she moved away. "No one needs to know." She winked.

"Thank you!"

The woman moved towards the other patient with a smile. "Tea, lovey?"

Sue was resolutely silent.

Emily crunched on her biscuit.

"Thanks again," she called out as the trolley was quietly wheeled away.

"There's some that's a pleasure to serve." The tea lady called out.

"Wow, she hates you already." Emily leaned down to Sue. "What did you say to her?"

"I was my usual affable self. I did tell her I wouldn't eat plain biscuits, for the money I'm paying here, I expected Tim Tams."

"Oh dear. Guess I got your biscuit stash for the day."

"The old bitch! I get sliced and diced and you score the goodies. Guess you did your Queen act?"

"What act is that?"

"Gracious to all and offensive to none."

"That's the one." Emily crunched on her second biscuit. She poured tea and held the saucer out.

Sue attempted to lift herself. She clung to the overhead railing, then collapsed back onto her pillow. "Through a straw, please."

"Poor you!" Emily sat back and watched as Sue attempted to sip her tea lying close to horizontal.

"That's determination for you. Anyone would think it was scotch the way you're swishing it down."

"Wish it was. What time is it?" Sue handed her tea cup back.

Emily noticed the deep lines around Sue's eyes and the thick sprigs of white hair close to her temple and ears. "Do you want to sleep? I can go."

"No, stay." Sue held her hand. "Do you know who called me before?"

Emily shook her head.

"Sam."

"What!"

"I know, I bumped into his sister in the corridor this morning. She was visiting her husband. I was jittery and said more than I intended to about why I was here. She must've called him."

"He still has your mobile number."

"I still have his."

"That's sweet. What did he say?"

Sue was silent for a moment. "At first, general stuff. He said he was sorry I needed surgery. Then we talked about work, mutual friends."

"And?"

"Nothing more. We didn't talk about us. It's been fifteen years. It would've been odd, even for us."

"How did he sound?"

"Good. Happy." Sue looked down and Emily saw a nerve pulse in her cheek.

"How were you?"

Sue traced a line on the sheet as she spoke. "Fine on the phone. When I got off, I burst into tears."

"Oh, Suzie."

"No, I'm fine now. It's been an emotional day and to hear his voice on top of that was too much."

Emily squeezed her hand but remained silent.

"I never told you why we broke up." Sue lowered her voice. "I broke his heart. He wanted a child and I didn't. I wanted to see the world, make a name for myself. Domestic bliss was never my goal. I wanted him to have the same dreams." She swallowed hard.

Emily listened.

"He asked me to go off the pill, so we'd try for a baby. I couldn't do it. I'd seen you up close with your babies and knew it wasn't for me. So I pretended to stop taking it. One day, he was searching for the headache tablets I always kept in my handbag and found the packet I was hiding. He was so hurt, he didn't speak to me for a week. We limped along for a year but he couldn't get over the deception. In hindsight, it was the end of us."

"What does he do now?"
"Still in management but in the field of sports therapy. He's married and has two kids, ten and eight years old."
The TV alongside increased in volume and Sue winced. "Not now." She leaned back on her pillows and turned her head to the side.
"I was never maternal." Sue spoke softly and Emily leaned over to catch her words. "I don't regret it at all, I've had an amazing career and life. But just imagine, he called today! I have a hysterectomy and remove organs that define my fertility and he calls the same day. Isn't life amazing?"
She turned to Emily. "Today, of all days."
The other occupant switched channels and another game show commenced, as bright and brassy as the first. Sue stared blankly at the screen, her eyes dark.
Emily held her hand and they quietly watched the TV together.

Chapter 19

"Sorry it's a weeknight catch up. Matt and I really need to pack tomorrow night, the removalists come first thing Saturday morning."

"You're not interrupting my social life."

"Dom, you don't have one."

"Not one I'd tell you about."

Emily and Matt sat at the table and listened to the sparring. She winked at him. "Adults, yet always children to me. "

Sarah sat straight backed, flicking her hair over her shoulders as she outlined her plans to Dominic. He sat opposite, a tangle of limbs and unruly curls, his brown eyes focused on her.

"Is it love?" Emily wondered, "or sorrow in those eyes? Our lives change again and he keeps his quiet counsel."

Sarah turned to Emily. "And I have work lined up. I've got four days at a primary school, as a couple of women are on maternity leave. Y'know, Mum, you could get a really nice house in Gosford with the sale price of this flat. It'd be a great sea change for you."

"And a great babysitting opportunity for you." Dominic observed.

"I'm not as mercenary as you. I didn't move back in with Mum when Matt and I broke up that time."

"Maybe you didn't feel it as much."

"That's rich, coming from you. I saw Jenny last week and she said you hadn't talked to each other in a month. Typical of you."

"And you know me so well."

Silence at the table.

"Great roast, Emily."

Emily laughed. "Thanks, Matt. There's nowhere to go after that conversation, is there?"

"Mum," Sarah leaned forward, "just so you know, Dad and Elspeth left for France last weekend."

"Oh."

"In case you tried calling him."

"Thanks."

"She was really excited. Elspeth hasn't been to France before."

Emily was silent.

"Dad let us stay in the townhouse while they're away. It's so nice to be in bigger space, have breakfast in a courtyard and not on a balcony. By the way, Mum, do you have the teak oil Dad asked you for? He's asked us to oil the antiques while they're gone."

"I'll get it now." Emily walked down the hallway.

Dominic murmured to Sarah. "You're as thick as Dad, no wonder you two are mates."

"It's better Mum knows. You hide things from her, treat her like a baby. I won't do that."

"Sarah, I don't know where it is," Emily came back to the table. "It must be in the garage. I'll look for it later."

"Do you remember the stuff in the attic?" Sarah nudged Dominic.

"At Strathfield? God yes, we had more up there than we had downstairs."

Emily sat up. "It didn't get in anyone's way."

Sarah leaned forward, her eyes lit up. "Dom and I used to go through the packing boxes when we were supposed to be practising."

"But I heard you both playing."

"Dom taped us. He'd play a tape and we'd turn the boxes upside down. Remember, Dom?"

He grinned.

"I thought Mum was preparing a dowry for me." Sarah laughed. "There was so much stuff up there, tea towels, table cloths, china, furniture. All packed away. It was like there was a secret family in the attic that used it."

"I've always hoarded things, get that from my mum."

"It was amazing." Dominic said. "We'd have tea parties with the china, then pack it away carefully just in case."

"There wasn't that much!"

"There was, Mum." Sarah interrupted. "Where did it all go in the divorce?"

"I took it. Don't you recognise the plates?"

Dominic and Sarah looked down. "Oh my God, it is too! At least you didn't have to buy new stuff for the flat."

"Just furniture."

"And it's not as if you left any plants behind either."

"What do you mean?"

"You and dad never planted anything in the garden. There were stacks of plants but they stayed in the plastic tubs they came in."

"That's right!" Sarah exclaimed, "when the backyard was emptied, I remember thinking how bare it looked. Not a shrub remained."

Emily shrugged. "I couldn't see the point of planting anything if we intended selling up when you kids moved out."

"Mum, you lived over twenty years in that house. My friends used to laugh about it when they visited. It was weird."

Dominic scooped the last ladle of risotto onto Matt's plate. "For you, man. You'll need all your strength, being at the mercy of Sarah's ambitions."

"We'll take Gosford on as a team."

"I think I've found where we want to buy." Sarah put her fork down. "Killcare Heights. It's absolutely gorgeous. We can just afford it with our deposit, though not a waterfront. We'll need two cars, which is a bummer."

"Team Sarah." Dominic murmured.

Matt laughed. "She can do the house thing, I don't mind."

"Prelude to total mind control. Let's take a beer out onto the balcony."

"Thanks for dinner, Emily."

Emily smiled as she watched them walk out. "Keep an eye on my fountain!"

She turned back. "Are you nervous, darling?"

Sarah looked at her blankly.

"About leaving Sydney."

"Why would I be?"

"I'd have been terrified. I had the two of you by your age and all I wanted was to have you both safe and settled. Anything else would've been a bonus."

"When did you and Dad buy the Strathfield house?"

"When he got his first Christmas bonus. A commercial for dog food. You were born the following year as a result of those dog biscuits."

"Did you want children?"

"Straight away. Your dad was great with kids, I'll give him that."

"Still is. He's hoping we start a family soon. Mum..."

"Yes?"

"Elspeth's still young enough to have a baby."

"My God, she isn't pregnant?"

"No." Sarah looked down at the table. "Not yet. She really wants one."

"Well, if you're really lucky, some nights you could babysit your uncle or aunt." She stood and commenced clearing the plates from the table. Her hands found it hard to grip the cutlery and she concentrated on one piece at a time.

Sarah moved across to the sofa and pulled her phone out. As she bent down, she stumbled and Emily saw her move a painting sideways, with a scowl.

She kept stacking plates, the order soothing her disquieted heart.

Chapter 20 - View 2

"Oh, my God, it's happened again!"

"Emms, it's 7 o'clock in the morning." Sue's voice was faint over the line. "Are you ok? The kids aren't sick? Bob hasn't found a newer, new woman?"

"I've got another date."

Silence on the line.

"Did you hear me, I'm going out with a man again."

"Is that it? I've just had a hysterectomy and I can barely speak."

"I need my touchstone."

Sigh on the line.

"Give me a minute to fluff my pillows."

Emily waited.

"What night are you seeing him?"

"Don't be ridiculous. We're going for a muffin this morning. He's another dog walker."

"What is it with you and dogs?"

"Mark asked me out for dinner but I suggested coffee. It's easier, I can bail early."

"Poor Stan."

"I know, it was so awkward, we were all standing together at the park when he asked me. Am I turning into a slut?"

"Yes, about time too."

"There's one problem."

"Mm?"

"He's handsome and has charisma overload. Like a nice version of Bob."

"Suck it up, girl. You need to find your best pair of track pants and I need to sleep. Wake me when you get back."

"I'm pathetic, aren't I?"

"Yes. Now go away."

Emily hung up the phone and surveyed the casual clothes strewn over the sofa. "Casual chic," she pondered "or not trying at all comfy?"

She grabbed the black track suit. "Matches the dark circles under my eyes," she mused.

Mimi was waiting in the front garden, with no sign of Sylvia in sight.

"Just you and me girl," Emily bent down to pat her, "Her Majesty slumbers on." She felt her hand tremble as she ruffled Mimi's fur. "From now on, you and I march around that park, no more socialising. You're not to stop or sniff a thing, do you hear me?"

Mimi whined as her collar was attached.

"Don't make me feel guilty."

They entered the park. Fallen leaves were underfoot and Mimi stopped to sniff a pile. Emily sighed and waited.

From across the walking track, she saw a man wave.

"Hey, Stan!"

He walked across, head bowed.

"You look tired. All ok with Alice?"

"She's not doing too well, refusing to eat or drink. They've got her on a drip. The kids are so upset, I don't know what to say anymore."

"I'm sorry to hear it. Is there something else the nursing staff can do?"

"Short of sedating her, no. That just aggravates the dementia."

"It's a cruel disease."

"The awful thing is, I don't mind the deterioration. At least I know what direction we're heading. I can see the end will come. That's an awful thing to say, isn't it?"

She squeezed his arm. "Not to me, or any of your friends."

Stan looked up as a tall, athletic man approached from the top hill. "Here's Mark. Enjoy your coffee."

"Come join us."

"Another time."

She watched him walk away, then braced herself.

"Good morning, Emily." Mark approached her and she raised her voice in response.

"Hi there!" She cursed herself as the words came out. "Too bright and cheery," she winced.

"Have you walked yet?"

"No, I just saw Stan as I came in. Mimi needs to run now, Elvis needs to leave the building." She winced again. "God, what I am saying?" she thought. She bent over to remove Mimi's collar and the movement steadied her hands.

"Shall we?"

They walked in silence awhile, as the dogs sprinted to a brace of trees on the hill ahead.

"I love the change of seasons." Emily motioned to the landscape. "The fresh air is irresistible."

"I can resist it." Mark replied. "I get hay-fever. Change of seasons is one big sneezefest for me." A sweep of grey hair fell over his face and Emily watched the attractive tilt of his head as he spoke.

"You're new here, aren't you?" The grey hair swept over again.

"About three months in Erskineville, I've bought a two bedder from my divorce settlement."

"Where were you before?"

"A house in Strathfield."

"It's a big adjustment, isn't it?"

"Yes!" She laughed. "My kids don't understand why I'm so tentative about things."

"I know, it needs to feel like home. You need to make connections with neighbours and local shopkeepers before it feels normal again. Kids can pick up and go but a home leaves a mark on an adult heart."

"How long have you been here?"

"Ten years, I have a townhouse in Enmore. I drive here because of the dog park."

"Does it feel like home?"

"Now it does, but it took a long time. Balmain will always be home to me, my ex-wife and I raised our kids there. When we split, I could've bought a one bedroom flat there but I didn't want to put the kids up on a sofa. Or share my room!" He grinned. "So I traded area for space."

"Budget didn't stretch to a bigger flat in Balmain?"

"Not without a mortgage and I wasn't up for that on top of school fees and maintenance."

"My ex husband lives there with his new wife."

"Ouch. What's she like?"

"Waist the size of a stretched toothpick. Obsessive exerciser, wears size eight on a fat day, can't cook."

"Whoa, stop there. I get it."

"I wasn't finished," Emily laughed, "I haven't told you about her cooking classes in Provence."

"Hate her?"

"No, in many ways she liberated me. We hadn't been in love for years and she finished us. I just don't know how to live the next bit of my life."

"You've started well, early morning walks with your dog."

"On loan."

"Still good for you. They're a social bunch here, aren't they? My work lets me start late some mornings, so it fits in nicely." He crouched down and called out "Rufus, over here." The collie bounded into his arms, barked, then sprang up the hill again.

"I think he smells a possum up that tree. The big doofus fancies himself a hunting dog."

"Mimi would lick a possum to death, especially if it were offering a croissant."

They walked behind the dogs and Emily glanced at Mark. He was the same height as Bob, but he walked with a slow, graceful gait.

"Bob was always in a hurry," she thought, "both in movement and conversation."

Mark tilted his head towards her as he spoke to her and she was becoming distracted by the wayward lock of grey hair.

"This walk clears my head for the day."

"You're a teacher, aren't you?"

"Yes. I have some really smart students this year. They're the ones I get up for." He leaned closer and the grey lock brushed his eyes. "Of course I have the idiot brigade as well, so its yin and yang."

"Lucky you. I work with a group of immature office girls, one of whom's in love with my son. It makes me realise how overrated youth is."

Mark laughed and clamped his hand on Emily's shoulder. "I know, I never understood middle aged men falling for younger women. The conversational barriers would kill me."

"I don't think they fall for the conversation. It's lust with a capital L."

"So cynical."

"So right."

He laughed again and she flushed with pleasure at the sound.

"Did you have a career before you had your kids?"

"I couldn't settle into a career. I flitted from job to job; first travel agencies, then hospitality, then bookkeeping. I was happy odd jobbing, it seemed to fit my personality type. I couldn't even finish university, I got halfway through, then tossed it in. Shame, really." She shook her head. "My son reminds me of myself. He changes jobs constantly, gives no evidence of having a career path. Must be genetic."

"Have you seen anyone post divorce?"

She shook her head.

"I didn't for ages either. Too busy picking up kids and ferrying them to sport. Then one day I thought stuff it, I'm up for it."

"And that was it for you?"

"Yup, I jumped back in the pool."

"I can't imagine it. I've been a wife and mother forever, its stamped on my forehead in indelible ink."

"Maybe we could try a non threatening date one night."

She quickened her pace. "I need my caffeine hit. Shall we?"

He let her lead the way.

"I bet you were a quiet wife."

She stopped walking. "Pardon?"

"You have a quiet way about you, quiet eyes... You observe, take note but keep your own counsel. I bet there were no histrionics when he decided to divorce you."

"How do you know he did?"

"I know."

She was silent.

"You don't always have to be quiet, Emily. It's ok to be loud sometimes. Y'know, when it counts." He looked ahead and yelled. "Rufus, come back. Dogs don't climb trees." He ran ahead and Emily watched as he restrained Rufus.

She followed behind, as Mimi ran back to her. "It's ok, girl, Rufus means no harm." She bent down to pat her.

……………………

Emily stood in the kitchen and stared at the board. She wrote in big letters: "Here's a second view of me, a woman with quiet eyes. Who needs to learn to be loud." She stared at the words, then turned away to get ready for work.

Chapter 21

"Suzie, get off that ladder!"

Sue turned around at the sound of Emily's voice and almost tripped over her flannelette pyjamas. "You weren't supposed to see this."

"Obviously. The convalescence must be over."

"I'm so bored, Emms. And I really needed to change the lightbulb."

"And you can't wait for me to help you? If you slip, your stitches will rip open, then where will you be?"

"In deep shit, waiting for you to rescue me."

"Then get down now."

Sue climbed down, admiring her handiwork as she stepped back. "Didn't hurt at all."

Her mobile sounded inside her pocket and she checked the message. "One moment." She paced her front garden as she punched a message into her phone. "I love lecturing the dickheads in my office via mobile. It's detached abuse. I'm so good at that."

Emily smiled. "C'mon, let's have tea, I need to fuss over someone. Dom walks around like a nervous shadow, Sarah breezes in and out. No one needs me."

Sue winced as she walked up the porch stairs. The pyjamas hung over her frame.

"You look like a convict wearing those striped jammies."

They entered the small lounge room and Sue sat gingerly on the sofa. She picked at the pattern and pointed to the faint stains on the fabric. "How many glasses of red wine have we consumed here, talking about the ills of humanity?"

"Too many." Emily filled the kettle. "And many more to come."

Sue was silent.

"Have you spoken to your specialist? Did he get the results of the biopsy?"

"He did."

Emily felt her hands tremble.

"The cancer has spread outside the cervix."

"Bugger. How far?"

"Not much." Sue straightened her back and Emily noticed the pallor of her skin. "Turns out I'll need chemoradiation, to knock it all out of me."

"Do it. I'll move in, cook and clean for you."

"Settle down. It's a couple of sessions, five minutes at a time. I might need help getting home, that's all."

"I can do that."

"Thanks. Where's my cuppa?"

"Coming."

Emily bit hard on her lip as she poured their tea. Sue sat cross-legged on the sofa, her head resting backwards. Her face a shimmery white under the fluorescent light.

"I haven't stopped thinking about Sam."

"You haven't talked about him in years."

"I know." Sue picked at a loose thread on the sofa. "We were together for twelve years. He was the love of my life."

Emily blinked hard as she approached with their mugs. "I didn't know."

"Neither did I." Sue sipped her tea. "We used to have pillow fights on a Saturday morning. Sam could be so silly and carefree, I really loved that about him." She was silent awhile. "After we broke up, I had a fling with an office colleague. The next morning, I tried to pillow fight with him and I was nearly sick with shame. I felt like I had violated a precious memory. I don't know why I'm rambling on like this."

Emily opened the cookie jar. "Illness can make you reflective, it's natural. You need a biscuit, it takes the edge of melancholia, I've discovered. And makes you prodigiously fat."

Sue laughed. "You would've been a great shrink."

"I'd have gone mad absorbing everyone's unhappiness."

"True."

Emily reached for the biggest cookie and shrugged at Sue's horrified look. "Do you regret not marrying Sam when he asked you?"

Sue crunched her biscuit. "Not at the time. I regretted he didn't love me enough to accept me as a free spirit."

"You sound like Dom, he said something similar about Jenny. I never had that fearlessness in me. Content to live a small life in the suburbs, raising 2.2 children."

"Do you have regrets?"

"Other than not leaving Bob first, no. I wouldn't change the life I had."

"Lucky you. I do. I regret having never been loved by a kindred spirit. Someone who loved my quirks. Ultimately, I drove Sam away and all I wanted to do was pull him close."

Emily put down her mug. "Here, give me your paddles. Time for a foot massage."

"Thanks, Emms." Sue lay horizontal, still crunching on her biscuit. "My mother would be horrified to see this. She believed standards had to be maintained."

"Don't we define ourselves by our mother's standards? Even if we hated them."

"Mmm."

"Are you in pain?"

"No, but I need another biscuit." Sue held out her hand.

Emily laughed. "Who knew that somewhere in that disciplined frame lurked a true piglet?"

"Indeed." Sue crunched on. "You've still got the magic touch."

"Not according to Bob."

"What did you love about him?"

"In the beginning?" Emily laughed. "That sounds biblical." She paused. "He was full of happy stories. When I was with him, I thought I would become part of them."

"Do you mean because of your weirdo family? That brother of yours..."

"I thought of Rodney the other day, wondered if he was still in Lismore."

"He never saw your parents again after he left home."

"No. Mum tried staying in touch but he never called her. Didn't come to their funerals either."

"It's amazing how much bad blood there can be in families. We never had that in my family, my parents were too dull to clash with."

"Lucky you." Emily looked up as bird song sounded from the window. A small, brown bird looked in at the sill, inquisitive eyes alight. In a quick flash of feathers, it was gone.

"I missed him when he left. I was twelve, just starting high school and suddenly I was an only child. I hated it." She stood abruptly. "Another cuppa?"

"Please." Sue sat up and held her abdomen as she did so. "Did Rodney ever say why he left? Was the fight between him and your Dad?"

"Of course. One humdinger when he was eighteen."

"What was it about?"

Emily turned to fill the kettle. "I don't remember."

"It's funny, isn't it." Sue placed a cushion behind her back. "You make a decision and it doesn't feel momentous at the time, yet it can reverberate your life long."

"You've got a bad case of reflectiveness."

"What's the cure, Doc?"

"More biscuits."

"No more. Got to maintain my figure. I'm going to die a size ten with full war paint on my deathbed. Maybe wearing a pair of kitten heels."

"Too soon to talk of death at our age."

"I've thought about it."

Emily turned to see Sue stare out the window. The light caught her forehead and Emily saw the faint scar that rimmed her upper right eyebrow.

"It's still there, Suzie," she spoke softly, "the scar from when we tried to wax your stray hairs off."

"We were fourteen going on four." Sue turned back to look at her.

"What did we know?"
"Not much."
"What do we know now?"
"Not much."

"Not to be morbid but I have thought of dying. I wondered who would come to my funeral, would Sam? Of course he would, he's that sort of man. And he'd tell his lovely wife, who would in turn completely understand."
"You did love him."
"Yes."
The bird had returned to the sill. It sang of love and death, with cocked head and swelled chest.
"I thought I would meet someone else. I was 35 years old and a remarkable man was just around the corner." Sue placed a cushion on her stomach and balanced her mug on top. "It's remarkable how few remarkable men there are. The ones I met were either running away from a marriage or boring careerists with no heart. It didn't take long for regret to set in."
"But you didn't want kids."
"No, I didn't. But in hindsight, maybe I could've done one."
Emily resumed massaging Sue's feet. "Hindsight, such a powerful thing."
"I start chemo next week."
"OK."
"I need to walk." Sue got to her feet slowly. "I feel like picking on my staff. Back in 5 minutes."
Emily watched her walk away.
She stared at the window sill, willing the small bird back. The ledge remained empty, the bird had completed its song for now.

Chapter 22

"Heavens, this place is huge!"

Sarah turned to her mother. "Erina Fair Mall? It isn't when you get used to it." She pursed her lips, staring at the long corridor spaces of the mall. "I need to find a cocktail dress. The Principal has organised a drinks night to welcome Matt." She stopped in front of a boutique. "Wait one minute."

Emily sat on the Ottoman at the shop entrance.

Sarah carried a black dress to the counter. "I'll take this one." She lay it on the counter. "I tried it on last week, I know you have a no return policy. No, don't tissue wrap it, just put it in a bag. Don't you have paper bags?" She leaned over to sign her name. "No, my signature never looks the same, it's me though." She motioned with her hand to Emily. "Let's go for coffee, it's on the way to the car. Follow me." Sarah strode ahead. She motioned to the outdoor cafe at the entrance. "Sit down, Mum. I'll order."

Emily watched her from her seat. "Is she mine?" she pondered. "Or did they mix up the babies at the maternity ward of the hospital, like I always suspected?"

Sarah flopped down. "I'm so tired, I haven't had a minute to myself since we moved here."

"Poor you. By the way, you were very bossy with the sales girl."

"No, I wasn't."

"I don't tell sales staff what shopping bags to keep in their stores."

Sarah was silent. She stirred sugar into her coffee, then rolled the sugar sachet in her hand, then unrolled it. Then rolled it again.

"You've done that since you were little."

Unexpectedly, Sarah's eyes glistened tears.

"Oh, darling, what's up?" Emily squeezed her hand. "I haven't upset you?"

"It's not you." She was silent again.

Emily formed sentences in her mind, poised to ask them, hesitated. She noticed Sarah's hands were trembling as she held her cup.

"Both my children are unknown to me." She mused.

Sarah wiped her eyes and looked around to see if anyone was staring. "Sorry about that." Sarah held her cup tightly. "I'm a bit overwhelmed at the moment. Since we've moved here, we just haven't stopped."

"Of course, darling, you're just feeling your way around."

"No, I'm not." Sarah stared directly at her. "People can take me or leave me. I don't care what anyone thinks."

"Of course."

"Stop saying that! You're always so diplomatic." Sarah drummed the table with her nails and Emily watched the tremor in her hands.

"Our neighbour's son plays drums in their garage, so we haven't had a proper sleep since we arrived. Matt's a bundle of nerves, trying to make a good impression and I'm.." She stopped and her eyes filled again. "I can't fall pregnant. We've been trying so hard and it just won't happen."

"You're under a lot of stress, darling. Maybe it's too soon, let yourself settle in to the new life you have up here. It all takes time."

"But you had the two of us by my age."

"That was the eighties. Smaller mortgages and less career stress than now."

Sarah twisted a length of her hair around her fingers. "I don't want to be an old mum. I just want it to happen now."

"It will, honey. It just takes time."

"If you think." Sarah leaned back. "Matt says I should chill too." She tore the rolled paper into shreds and opened another sugar sachet.

"Sarah, you were never interested in kids before. Is Matt so keen?"

Sarah looked away. "Desperate to be a dad. And a high school principal within six years."

"You'd never guess from looking at him that he's ambitious."

"He's worse than I am. Matt maps out five year plans and sticks to them. I love that about him, it makes me feel safe."

"Your Dad and I didn't do such a good job of that."

"It was pretty good at home for a long time. Dad always chased a bit of skirt, Dom and I knew that. He used to flirt with the teachers at school at parent-teacher night." She shuddered. "Used to make me feel icky in class afterwards. Elspeth will notice it one day, he can't help himself."

Emily noticed Sarah's tired eyes. "As long as you're not sacrificing your dreams for Matt."

"As if, Mum. That was your generation." She paused. "I'm horrible to you, I know. It's like with Dom, we pull each other apart, just out of habit." She rubbed her eyes. "Some days, I'm tired of the game. I wonder if Matt and I will turn on each other, the way I do with you two."

Emily smiled. "I'm made of tough stuff, so's Dom." She stroked Sarah's arm. "Are you happy with the villa?"

"It's bloody isolated, I can't walk to the local shops or pop down the street for a coffee. Bit like living in a retirement village. There's no one about at night either. I can't wait till we move to our own place. I'll be fine then, more families about."

"Just don't rush that."

"We can't, we've a six month lease."

"Good. Do you hear from your girlfriends?"

Sarah's beautiful eyes looked introspective. "We text. I didn't realise how much I'd miss them. I can't drop by for a chat or go out to the movies with them spontaneously now. I didn't expect to feel that." She rolled the sugar sachet in her hands, the small grains spilled out of the torn paper and formed white swirls on the table. "That's about the only thing I didn't factor into the move, girlfriend-sickness. It takes time to make those sorts of friendships." She squared her shoulders. "But I will. One school is promising, I've met a couple of people I really like. It'll work out."

"Of course it will, darling.."

Sarah stood. "Let's go. Matt will be home by 5 and we like to walk before dark."

"Of course." Emily stopped at the expression. "Sorry, old habits die hard."

Sarah stared down at her.

"If you're going to start editing my language, I'll be afraid to speak. Between you and Sylvia, I'll always be on my guard."

"The old lady picks on you too? That's sad." Sarah gazed at her. "You're still dog walking?"

Emily nodded. "I've had coffee with two men through it."

"Really?"

"Yes, I'm meeting a fabulous set of people already. I'm starting to settle into my home."

"I can imagine. Chained to Dom and a spoilt hound."

"Sarah! You can be so negative, just like your dad. Stop labelling me, it's so annoying."

"You never criticise Dom the way you do me."

"What do you mean?"

"His way of communicating with people. I'm demanding, yet he's perfect in your eyes."

"That's not true. I love you both equally."

"You may but you're softer on him. He's like the runt of the pack, weak and ineffectual yet you never point that out. My flaws are open season; however. I can't be like him and I don't want to."

"I'm not asking you to."

"I see it in your eyes when you're with him. You laugh at his weird jokes, never criticise his running away from things."

"Sarah, Dom's more like me. He's humble and unsure. We have a similar sense of humour, that's all."

"Really." Sarah walked ahead of her. "It's probably better you go home tonight, rather than sleep over. You'll be against traffic at least."

"Of course." Emily replied.

Sarah was silent as they walked back to the car.

Chapter 23

"You look like you could use a kip." Sylvia handed Emily a tea cup. "Not sleeping well?"

"My kids are worrying me. My daughter's moved to the Central Coast and my son's having a nervous breakdown."

"Children are meant to worry you. My sister worried about her son till her deathbed. Look where that got her."

Emily laughed.

"How is your sick friend?"

"Starting chemo tomorrow. I'll collect her from the hospital."

"My mother went with cancer, poor thing. My father believed she never got over the flooding of old Adaminaby."

"Was it so nice?"

"Just a small country town but it was home to her. She said when she looked at Lake Eucumbene, it was like looking at ghosts. She would imagine the old buildings underneath. Used to give her the shivers."

"Must've been hard on the old folk of the town."

"It was strange. John Edward and I came down to see it soon after the flooding. Quite took my breath away." Sylvia fed Mimi a biscuit. "John Edward said there was no point moping, so he hired a tinny and we went fishing on the lake. Caught three trout on the first day, we think over the old bakery. John Edward wanted to catch one over the bank; said they'd lorded it over his family for years and he wanted payback. Men can be perverse, can't they?"

Emily laughed. "Yes, indeed. He was obviously a pragmatic man."

"Very. Apart from his poetic streak but I put that down to his parents. After we settled in Sydney, he stopped reading poetry. Said he couldn't read in the suburbs, he needed space to say the words aloud. John Edward believed true beauty was natural, not man made. He hated me wearing makeup."

"Must've been quite a character."

"Not to look at him. Oh, he was tall and handsome all right, but quiet and careful in all he did. Said I was the light of his life. Mind you, he wasn't a complete Nancy, he could ride a mean horse, too."

Sylvia's hands clasped tight as she sat within her memories.

"Did you ride together?"

Sylvia snorted. "Did we what! We galloped through the valleys the summer before he was sent away. It was an exceptional time to be young. We knew it could be our last summer together, so everything seemed fresh, yet so fragile. We took risks because we didn't know if we would live to take other risks together. Rode like maniacs through the bush, careered off our horses and came up laughing. No helmets to break our fall, just prayer and a belief that God would serve us as we'd serve our country."

Emily watched as the blaze faded from her eyes.

"Some of the young men we rode with that summer didn't come back. Young Bob McDougall died in the trenches in France. His girl, I don't remember her name, she never married. Wore her engagement ring around her neck and never left home. So many lives lost, so we felt blessed. We were gifted by the Lord with time."

"Did John Edward get on with your parents?"

"Of course, they were solid people. My father would have loved him to work the land with him but Johnny wanted to see the world first. So many boys thought the war a great adventure. Father knew what he was in for."

Emily broke a biscuit. "Over here, Mimi, you big pudding."

Mimi shuffled over and devoured the offering.

"I'm surprised you didn't move back to Yalinda when you lost him."

"The only place I could visit family by then was in the cemetery. To build on the land we'd bought seemed daunting on my own, I didn't know if my health would hold up and how I'd cope if it didn't." She smiled. "See, I got soft living in the city, all the wonderful services it provides."

Emily laughed. "But you make a point of not using any, not even Meals on Wheels."

"That's for old people. Mother always said to leave charity for the disadvantaged and muster on as long as you can."

"I could collect your groceries..."

"No, thank you, I catch a bus and order home delivery. Keeps me in the world. If I were trapped at home, I'd go soft. John Edward said independence kept your mind sharp. Poor you, listening to the ramblings of an old woman."

Emily looked out to the garden. It was soaked with recent rain, the grass wild in patches. Small branches lay strewn on the lawn, the wood rotting into the soil.

"I love the smell of rain." Sylvia spoke. "When did you lose your parents?"

"I lost Mum a few years ago and my dad over twenty. He didn't know my kids."

"What a shame for them. A grandfather is special."

"Depends on the man."

"Mine was extraordinary. Self taught iron monger and great bushman. He taught me to ride. Bareback. Said the only way to understand a horse was to ride it as God made it, feel its power beneath you. I thought he was Banjo Paterson reincarnated."

"Must have been a lovely childhood."

"It was a hard one. My parents went to bed at sundown and were up at sunrise. They were worn out at sixty. We did as we were told and were God fearing. Seems the kids of today have so many choices, they're sabotaged by them. My life was a straight line on the station, I went to school and did my chores." She shook her head. "When I met John Edward, my path opened up. I knew my old life was over."

"Was it a shock, living in the suburbs?"

"At first, yes. But we were excited to have our own home." She looked ahead. "The only times I felt isolated was at night. I missed seeing the constellations in a country sky. That glorious darkness, lit with white stars. I missed the smell of the fields at night and gum leaves after rain. Sometimes, you need a brisk walk to still your heart. I couldn't still mine in the city, I was galloping everywhere with my thoughts at times. John Edward sat with me on the porch until it passed. He said it was the Sylvan Sylvie constellation passing through my heart, or some such nonsense." She bent her head and Emily watched her eyes darken.

They were silent awhile.

"It's getting cooler out here," Sylvia straightened her back. "And you, how did you meet your fella?"

"Very prosaic. An office romance. We went to the pub on Friday nights. Bob was a storyteller, he was always in the thick of it at the bar, swapping stories about clients and escapades he had as a kid. He grew up in the Southern Highlands and boarded in Sydney as a school kid. I thought he was full of fun and a good man. He liked me because I listened to him, that's what I did best in those days." Emily shook her head. "But his parents weren't as welcoming as your family were, so we felt united by their dislike of me. Us against the world, so to speak. My mum was a single parent and they didn't like to be associated with a broken home."

Sylvia nodded. "Country people can be suspicious. When I'd return to Yalinda, I'd get cut down real quick if I talked of town plays and opera. I learned to separate my two lives. John Edward advised me to do that, to keep friendly with our old crowd. Life's a compromise."

Emily looked at the wattle tree hanging over the front fence, imagining a tall, black haired man planting the first cutting. Beside him, a small, vivacious young woman turned the soil. They smiled at each other and he kissed the top of her head. She could see them, just as they were.

....

Emily stood in her kitchen that night, chalk in her hand as she pondered the chalk board. She reached up and wrote: "What a beautiful thing it must be to be young and lit with dreams."

Chapter 24

Emily bent over the new photocopier and examined the red warning light. Switched the power button off. On again.

The red light came on again.

"God, you make my life so hard," she muttered, "what was so wrong with the old photocopier?"

"Are you done?"

Emily started. "Serena, where did you creep up from?"

"I work here, remember?" The young woman eyed her. "You've lost weight. You're seeing someone!"

Emily bent towards her. "I did have coffee with a divine man the other day." She looked down. "Do you really think I've lost weight?"

"Definitely. Your waist tyre is gone." She pushed a wayward curl over her shoulder. "I don't know why women let themselves go after 40."

"Have a couple of kids, then come back and talk to me." Emily turned back to the photocopier and sighed. "Stop flashing at me!"

Serena moved her to one side. "You just have to re-set the paper size. Someone used A3 before you."

"You make it sound so easy."

"You make it sound so hard."

"Look, I'm not as technology literate as your generation."

"Stone age Emily."

Emily fantasied about dropping the photocopier on Serena's head.

"So, stone age Emily, are you ever gonna progress from coffee dates to dinner dates? Wear a dress, some lipstick even."

Emily stared at her, furious.

"Someone's got to get you back into the game. Your girlfriends obviously don't have a clue. Stop wearing nanna black for one thing. There's a whole colour spectrum out there and you don't use it."

She pointed to the photocopier. "Have you finished with it, because I need to get some advertising brochures out by this afternoon."

Emily stood aside in silence.

"Call the divine man to go out for dinner. You've got nothing to lose."

"More advice."

Serena flung a curl over her shoulder. "I'm not just good with photocopiers."

"So I see."

Serena printed her copies quickly and smiled as she left.

Emily lifted the lid of the copier and muttered. "Don't do anything to annoy me or I'll throw that skinny blonde at you." She pressed the copy button and waited.

Chapter 25

"Susie, are you meant to wash chemo down with red wine?"

"Buggered if I know." Sue sat on Emily's balcony, a throw rug over her legs. "It's nice out here, these outdoor seats are comfy."

"Don't fall asleep, OK? You're too heavy to lug to the car and I don't want you snoring on my balcony and disturbing my neighbour. She's on the committee. And the size of a blue whale."

"Oh dear." Sue giggled. She stood, leaned over the balcony and peered down. "What's that annoying sound?"

Emily looked in the direction of her wildly tilting glass. "Our new fountain. Isn't it lovely?"

"Darling." Sue held onto the railing tightly. "I don't feel too bad. I'm sure I could go back to work next week."

Emily laughed. "You only started chemo three hours ago! Listen to your good Scottish specialist."

Sue was silent awhile, staring down at the grounds. "They're starting to forget me."

Emily listened.

"Peter doesn't call every day now. He's grown in confidence since I've left and hires the big positions with the CEO. He's on half my salary, so they could replace me."

"You haven't heard anything?"

"No." Sue lifted the wine bottle and refilled her glass. "This is positively medicinal. You?"

"Why not?" Emily held out her glass.

"It's not that I need the money now. My mortgage is minimal and I can afford a less stressful job." She looked directly at Emily. "But this is who I am, what I've worked for. I'm used to people jumping at the sound of my voice, I've grown used to the deference! I don't want to give up that part of my life up. Not now."

"You'll always be a personality type A, to me."

"Thank you. I think."

Emily stood alongside her at the railing and pointed upwards. "Look at those magnificent stars. Been there for thousands of years and I've only just noticed them tonight. Wouldn't you love to see them in a country sky?"

"No." Sue burped. "Excuse me, I don't know where that came from." She sipped her wine. "I should re-arrange my life during this time. Minimise my stress."

Emily leaned closer to hear the soft words.

"But if I do that, I lose the reason I gave up Sam. It would all be pointless, you see? Like the universe laughing at me. What a fool you are, you choose the path that left you alone and unloved."

Emily hugged her. "You still have me."

"Thank God." Sue wiped her eyes. "Must be a side effect of chemo. I never cry." She cocked her head to one side. "You live in the noisiest apartment block. What's that racket?"

Emily laughed. "Sylvia's record player. When she's feeling feisty, she plays 'Carmen' at full tilt."

"Spiteful old bag."

"She isn't, she's of a different era. Underneath her frail persona, is a woman who truly loved and was loved in return. Like a muse to a long gone artist."

"Did you just say what I thought you did?"

Emily giggled. "I'm on my third glass. I lost coherency on number two. Top up?"

"Absolutely."

"You don't think I'll accidentally kill you? How will I explain that to your specialist?"

"Science experiment gone wrong. He'll admire you for it. God, I love red wine." Sue leaned over the balcony again. "You've got possums down there. I can see them, size of miniature ponies."

"You're drunker than I am!" Emily staggered to the balcony and gazed down. "I can't see a thing without my glasses." She fell backwards and landed neatly in a chair.

"Oh, look, Suzie, the bottle's empty! I'll get another one."

"Good girl." Sue peered down, trying to focus on a darkened area of the lawn. "I can see the little bastards." She called out. "Stop eating the bushes! Bad possum!" She stumbled and Emily caught her on her return.

"Don't jump!"

"Don't be ridiculous! I was lecturing the possums."

"And you call me ridiculous. Did they answer you?" Emily set a bottle on the table. "This is part of Dom's stash. I really shouldn't."

"Bloody oath you should." Sue uncorked the bottle and filled their glasses. "Not bad."

They sat down again and drank in silence awhile.

"How did Bob make you feel?"

"Before I grew to hate him?"

"Yep, then."

Emily was silent.

"Waiting."

"He wasn't like Sam. I wasn't like you."

"Still waiting."

"Piss off, Suzie."

Sue sat upright. "My God, did you hear that?" She peered over the railing. "Look! That wasn't on the grass before."

"Let me get my glasses. And a torch." Emily swayed as she walked across to the coffee table.

Sue leaned over the balcony and pointed. "Look at that."

Emily clutched her cardigan as she looked in the direction of Sue's wildly pointing hand.

"Oh, my God, it's a dead possum!"

"No it's not, you silly woman. Put your glasses on."

"I thought I did. Oh, look at that, I'm still holding them." Emily whistled as she examined the scene near the fountain. "It's even worse, it's a dead cherub! Let's go down and investigate."

"Should I be scared?"

"Of statues? You are drunk, Suzie." Emily tugged her. "Follow me. Just leave your wine glass here." She giggled. "Remember the night we got drunk on the bottle of Baileys we stole out of your dad's drinks cabinet? We must've had a thimble each."

"We were fifteen, Emms. It didn't take much back then."
"Shh!" Emily held her hand to her lips. "Let's see if we can catch the culprits. Remember, silence a la morte."
"Are you channelling Sherlock Holmes?"
"Shh!" Emily tiptoed down the entrance stairs and opened the security door. She flashed the torch over the lawn and listened.
Sue staggered behind her. "I feel shocking." She held onto Emily's shoulder. "I think you've killed me."
"Shh, Suzie, this is important." Emily shone the torch over the lawn again. "Can't see a thing." She shone the torch over the fountain. "Oh my Lord, they've done it again." She ran to the fountain. "Look, they've broken off both arms."
"That's a feral possum!"
"It's someone in my complex. Violent criminals, the lot of them."
Sue looked around apprehensively. "I think I preferred the possum option. Let's go back to your flat, it's a bit chilly down here."

Emily felt in her pocket. "Oh, no!"
"I don't like the sound of that."
"Well you did insist on getting me drunk. I can't help it if I forgot my keys."
"Shit." Sue looked pitiful. "And I've just had chemotherapy. I really am going to die tonight."
"Don't be ridiculous. Here, take my jumper. Let's lie on the grass, alongside the poor wee arms." Emily patted the grass alongside her. "See, we can admire the night sky. Dom will be home before midnight."
Sue whimpered.
"Not such a corporate woman now are we, lamb chops?"
Sue lay gingerly on the grass. "I feel shocking."
They stared at each other and burst out laughing.
"You owe me an answer, at least."

Emily turned to her.

"The Bob question."

"Oh." Emily stared upwards as she replied. "He made me feel secure."

"Really?"

"Financially secure. Emotionally, I was shut down. I married him because I didn't love him. If you marry someone you love, they can hurt you. If you marry someone you have regard for, they can never really touch you with their words or actions. It was better that way for me."

Emily turned to her. "You're shocked. I had my reasons. Bob got a stable home, two beautiful kids. Many women live like that."

"I guess." Sue replied. "Look how bright that star is!" She shivered and pulled the cardigan closer to her. "A night of surprises."

Sylvia's record player had stopped. The only sound was the gentle splash of the fountain.

"Definitely a night of surprises."

Chapter 26

"Good morning, honey." Emily turned as Dominic walked out onto the balcony. "Thanks for rescuing us last night."

"More like resuscitating! I thought she was dead."

"It would take more than two bottles to kill Suzie. I should give her a call."

"Let her sleep. She didn't get to bed until after 1am. Took me half an hour to wake her in the car."

Emily laughed. Out of the corner of her eye, she spied Cecilia standing at the fountain with her husband.

"Look, Dom, they're at the scene of the murder."

"Not again?"

"Yes." She moved backwards instinctively.

Dominic draped his limbs around an outdoor chair and Emily observed him. His frame was thinner.

"You need a haircut, darling. Let's go for coffee at the bakery." She tapped his arm. "Some fresh air will do us both good." He followed her silently.

Emily tilted her head to the sunlight as she exited the apartment block. A gentle autumnal breeze lifted foliage and shook flowers.

"Can you believe it?" Emily's arm was seized from behind her and she winced.

"Ouch. Oh, Cecilia, it's you." She stared at the watery, blue eyes in front of her. "I know, I saw it last night." Then bit her lip.

"Saw who did it? Was it that fat cow, Rhonda? I'll sue her."

"I mean, I saw the damage last night. I had a friend over and we were sitting on the balcony, chatting. She thought she heard a noise, so we investigated."

"Was that you singing and laughing last night?"

"We were a bit tanked. Chemotherapy and red wine don't mix."

"Did you see anything?"

"Nothing I remember clearly."

Dominic snorted.

Emily tried to pull her arm away.

"She always gets away with it." Cecilia muttered. "I've rung Gus, he'll come down soon. I'm really quite distressed about it." She eyed Dominic as he stood in the background.

"My son." Emily spoke. "Dominic, this is Cecilia."

"Shame about your cherub."

"Thank you." Cecilia continued to eye him and he took a step forward.

"It's an amazing statue. I mean what's left of it. You must have eclectic taste."

Cecilia turned to her husband. "Take some photos. No, leave the arms where they are, when the police arrive, they can construct a crime scene. She's not going to get away with this."

Emily and Dominic tiptoed past them as Cecilia directed her husband's attention to the angles she wanted.

"I'm amazed she didn't fingerprint me." Dominic spoke when they were out of earshot. "I've got stubble on my chin, so I must look suspicious."

"And you've got an old lush for a mother. Guilt by association." Emily shrugged. "We weren't that loud last night."

"You were singing Bruce Springsteen when I arrived home."

"Oh dear. Which song? I only do a decent version of 'Born to run.'"

"In your opinion."

"Woops."

They crossed the road and watched as a police car parked in front of the apartment block. "Enjoy, boys." Emily murmured.

Dominic lifted a flower from a hedge and presented it to Emily.

"Thanks, darling."

"You never sang at home." He collected a flower for himself and placed it in the buttonhole of his vest. "Sarah said you sang her lullabies as a kid but I don't remember any."

"I'd given up by the time you were born. Your dad didn't like them."

"Bugger him. She loved them."

"Did she? She never said so."

He leaned over and hugged her. "It was good to hear you laughing last night."

"Thanks, son."

He adjusted his stride to hers and they walked in silence.

Ahead, a brown haired girl walked towards them. Dominic stopped in his tracks at the sight of her. She walked with a young man and they chatted animatedly.

"Dom!" She stared and ran to greet him. "I didn't know you'd moved to Erskineville. Hey, Emily."

"Jenny, darling, how good to see you." She kissed her, felt the fresh scent of her skin.

"I've moved in with mum till I find a new place."

Jenny flushed. "Oh. Meet my brother, Tim. He's just moved back from WA."

They shook hands. "Hey man, I've heard a lot about you."

"Ditto."

Jenny spoke quietly. "I heard you sold the house, Emily. Do you like your flat?"

"It's a work in progress. Some days I quite like it. Where did you move to?"

A pause.

"Closer to the city. I'm flat sharing till I decide where to move to next."

"Good idea."

"Good luck in Sydney." Dominic smiled at Tim.

"Thanks, man."

A step backwards. "Well, good to see you, Dom."

A smile and she moved away.

Dominic stared as they walked on.

Emily held his arm. "C'mon, we need coffee."

He was silent as they crossed the road to the cafe.

"Her brother looks nice."

He nodded.

"I feel for you, Dom."

He looked away. "I found out she's seeing someone else. I'm replaced already."

"Maybe that's her way of handling it, getting out and having fun. You should too."

"If I loved her less, sure."

"Sweet boy. It will take a while but it will hurt less eventually."

"Words of maternal wisdom."

"That's all I have. Sorry."

"Don't be. I'm in a shit mood, whatever you say, I'll twist."

"Not tempted to run after her and drop down on one knee?"

"What do you think?"

"I think we've just asked two rhetorical questions. Ah, here's the waitress."

As Emily ordered, she glanced at Dominic. He looked pallid, the lightness of youth erased in one swift blow.

"I've booked a ticket to South America."

She stared at him.

"Three weeks over the Christmas holidays. I've heaps of leave."

"Where?"

"All over, especially down south."

"Not Colombia?"

"Hitch-hiking through it. Mum, you've gone white! I was kidding."

"Not funny, Dom. I was imagining you in a bath of ice, with your kidneys ripped out and an IV hanging off your arm."

"That's a big leap from a backpacking holiday."

"Why not Fiji over Christmas? Worst thing that could happen is another military coup."

"Or a tsunami. Mum, stop worrying. You overanalyzed everything when we were kids. There was no spontaneity living with you."

"Your dad said the same thing."

"Well, he's a jerk."

"He's your dad."

"He can be both."

They grinned at each other.

"Do you remember once when I was little, I caught you crying in the back garden?"

Emily stiffened.

"I was so angry Dad made you cry, I offered you my Tonka truck to play with."

"I remember."

"I thought you were going to leave us. You were stacking all the plastic pots close together, I thought you were getting ready to move out. That's why I gave you the truck, to give you a reason to stay."

"I'd never leave you kids behind."

He caught her in a loose hug. She felt the touch of his dry warmth against her skin.

"Sarah and I remember that after you and Dad argued, you'd disappear to the attic. We'd hear banging noises and boxes being moved around. Sarah thought you were feeding the secret family. What were you doing?"

She looked away. "Stress release. I just re-organised the attic. Clean house, clean mind."

He nodded and held her close, then let go.

"I gotta go. I'm going to pick up a second hand copy of Lonely Planet. There's a section on how to survive South America with your vital organs intact."

She watched him cross the road and amble back to the flat.

In the sunshine, he looked less frail, less weighed down by loss.

Chapter 27- Round 3

Cecilia looked dishevelled.

Gus spoke. "This is long past a joke."

Flossie waved her knitting needles as she spoke. "I miss it. How long will it be in for repairs this time, Cecilia?"

"I don't know." Cecilia paused. "It may be weeks. Luigi's very busy, repairs are a sideline of his business. He chisels marble tombstones by trade."

The needles clicked on. "Too many dead people."

Rhonda was silent and Emily appraised her. "She looks so calm, she couldn't have done it," she reflected, "I'd have guilt stamped all over me if it were me."

"Rhonda."

Emily jumped as Cecilia spoke. "Gus and I have agreed that the Owners Corp will pay for its repairs. Again. Have you any ideas how we can make it safer for my little statue? You're the only one not to venture any thoughts."

"Well, Emily's pretty silent too. As usual." Rhonda's chins wobbled as she spoke. "It's sad, Cecilia, but we have to admit defeat. Those street kids have it in for the dear little thing. It's costing a fortune to repair and it's creating a backlog in the tombstone industry."

Emily watched as Cecilia tried to frown. A muscle in her forehead attempted to twitch, then stalled.

Cecilia spoke. "It's like living in a war zone here and we're not giving in. We said a year and a year it is."

Rhonda rolled her eyes. "Regardless of what it costs us."

Gus interjected. "Cecilia's right. I hate the thing but it got the majority vote. Let's fix it and hope for the best."

"Thank you, Gussy."

Cecilia turned her faded, cornflower blue eyes on Emily. "Did you see anything at all that night? You were so close."

Emily shook her head.

"I heard you both on the balcony." Rhonda leaned forward. "You're friend has a potty mouth." Her chins wagged in Emily's face. "Or was that you?"

"Sue heard a noise and saw something. I doubt she'd remember anything that would help us."

"Strange," Rhonda murmured, "how this happens after you and your son move in. He doesn't look like he's seen a razor in a while."

Silence.

"Stranger yet," she continued on, "you were caught beside the fountain, intoxicated beyond coherent speech; and yet I get implicated by Cecilia."

Gus interrupted. "No one's accusing anyone of anything. We've got to stay united or we'll succumb to in fighting and rumour-mongering."

"How much is the repair costing?" Rhonda looked across at Gus.

"About $500.00." Gus was sombre. "There were so many fragments on the grass, we were on our knees for an hour picking them all up."

"The Pieta." Emily spoke up, "you should leave a chip as an acknowledgement of the attack."

They stared at her.

"Never mind."

"We've contacted the police," Gus waved his clip board, "they wrote an incident report."

Flossie's needles clattered to a halt. "This is getting serious."

"Darn right it is. Damage to private property." Cecilia's cheeks were flushed. "Perhaps we should fence it off."

Gus and Rhonda glanced at each other. "That's not going to happen."

"You haven't invested in it like I have."

"We're certainly starting to." Gus muttered.

Cecilia focussed on Emily. "What does your son do? He leaves very early for work."

"He works for an IT company, they work on a roster system. Why?"

"I just wondered. I see him of a morning lurking in the dark."

Rhonda interrupted. "Are you spying, Cecilia?"

"I meditate on my balcony of a morning, it sets my mind for the day."

"So we shell out $500.00 for the repairs, on top of $1500 for its installation. Should we set up a retirement fund for it as well?"

"I've heard enough, Rhonda." Cecilia stood. "Gus, we should try a Skype meeting next time. I think it will be more civil."

"That's absurd, we live within metres of each other. Just because you skype your daughter in London doesn't mean you can order everyone else to do the same."

"Yes, suck it up, Cecilia." Rhonda added.

Cecilia left without another word.

Flossie's needles clattered. "Oh dear," she whispered, "she's really offended now!"

"Who cares?" Rhonda spoke loudly. "Stuck up bitch. She should've stayed on the other side of the bridge. I'm so tired of hearing about her lower North Shore friends." She stood and stretched her massive arms. "I respect the Committee's decision. I'm done with this."

As she swept past Emily, she bent down low to her. "I loathe Bruce Springsteen."

Chapter 28

They stretched out in the sun. Emily rolled her jeans up and examined her legs. "Do you remember, Suzie, how we sun-baked every afternoon after school? I'm paying for it now in age spots and wrinkles."

"It was worth it at the time." Sue stared across the park. "So this is the mutt park. No hot men here."

"Hot free zone. I think they have it on a sign somewhere." Emily sighed.

"At the risk of sounding ironic, because I'm the one going through chemo, are you alright?"

Emily sat up and hugged her knees. "I'm in a rut, six months into my new life. I feel hemmed in by Dom, my neighbours, Mimi. I don't look for responsibilities, they come yapping after me."

"Martyr trait?"

"I'm sorry I started this conversation."

"Now, don't get tetchy. You do have a tendency to sacrifice yourself to the altar of usefulness. Drop a few things, like walking that ridiculous dog."

"I can't."

"Kick Dom out, tell him to find his own place."

"I can't."

"Don't have afternoon tea every week at the old lady's house. Tell her you're busy."

"I can't."

They eyed each other.

"Hang some picture frames, make something permanent in your life."

"I can't."

Slow smile at each other.

"If I wasn't so tired, I'd tell you off. Get some spirit, blah, blah, blah..."

"I can't." Emily lay down again. "I'm filling in my days, just like I did with Bob, so I don't have to think. If I'm busy, I don't feel."

"I didn't realise how much your marriage defined you."

"Neither did I. After I had coffee with Mark, I realised I could start again, find a new partner." She looked directly into Sue's eyes. "But it's like I don't care about anything and I don't want to."

"I think it's healthy to take time for yourself."

"It frightens me to be still." Emily whispered.

"Why, blossie?"

"Because I'll get caught." Emily laughed. "What am I talking about?"

Sue stretched out. "I can do nothing very well."

"I never learned that skill. My mum was always busy, she didn't feel safe being still."

"Because of your dad?"

"What!"

"I've always wondered about him, Emms. He looked like a volcano about to erupt. And that was on a good day."

"He was just moody."

"Do you remember I came home with you once after school? Your dad was home. He looked so angry I was there, I thought he was going to hit your mum when she offered me afternoon tea."

"I don't remember that." Emily stood and brushed grass from her jeans. "Are you up for a stroll?"

"Of course."

They walked arm in arm. Emily noticed a tremor in Sue's arm and she held her tighter. "Darling friend," she thought, "stay with me." The tremor increased as they walked the circumference of the park's boundaries.

"I've been offered another job."

"You can pick your moments."

"No, I've been head-hunted."

Sue winced and Emily motioned to a bench. "Let's sit, I think you've had enough for one day."

"We'll end up two old ladies on a park bench. If we start fossicking in garbage bins, it's time to worry."

"What's the job?"

"Human Resources Manager of a not for profit organisation. Deals with placement of people on long term welfare into employment training programs."

"Suzie, in a million years, I couldn't see you do that."

"I know." Sue tilted her face to the sun. "I've met the CEO who runs it, I placed her brother in a position in our company. Lovely person, determined to make a difference. I remember thinking how futile her job was, working with losers."

"I hope you didn't say that to her."

"Emms, you know I don't have to say something to get my view across."

"Oh dear."

"Indeed. Anyway, she called me. Had heard I was sick and wondered if I wanted a change of direction. Y'know move from egocentric, high paying job to worthwhile but meagre paying, save the world job, in the remaining short time I have left on Earth."

"Did she really say that?"

"No, but you know how you don't necessarily have to say something to get your view across?"

They laughed.

"Are you interested?"

"No! Bunch of tossers." She was silent awhile. "I feel like I've lost control of my body." Sue held her arm up. "Look at the needle marks! And this is only the start. People are making calls on my body and I hate it. Can't change it though, because I don't have the expertise to make a good call myself."

"But you've researched the treatment options, you're in the loop."

"Yeah sure, but then you just go with your what your specialist says because you like the kind twinkle in his eyes."

"And the tartan bow-tie."

"That too." Sue turned to her. "It's not true they're all tossers. I was invited to a function last year. Bunch of decent people drinking white wine and me longing for a bloody Mary! They were all quietly spoken, amusing, focussed, not driven by the dollar. Everything I'm not. Everything that Sam stood for and I rejected. Marie, that's the CEO's name, made such a lovely speech. She said she came to a point in her career where she didn't want to make bucket loads of money for a big organisation, she wanted to change a life, one simple human life, for the better. I remember laughing at her inside, thinking what a wanker she was. Today, I'm not so sure who the wanker was."

"You're at crossroads, just like me. Regret is easy when you're down but the choices you made were important to you then. Remember visiting me when the kids were little and Bob was behaving like a bastard? I could see on your face that you knew you'd made the right choice. Hang onto that."
"Bob was a real shit to you."
"I thought I deserved it."
Sue sighed.
Emily nudged her. "My melancholia is contagious."
Sue clutched her arm. "Oh my God, I do have one piece of hot gossip. I bumped into Diane and Roger last week."
"No! Is he as gorgeous as ever?"
"Totally. She really married up."
"I know, lucky girl. They stayed married all these years."
"And still seem to love each other."
"Nauseating how well life turned out for her, she was such a cow at school. Does she look old?"
"Older than us, yes."
"Small mercies. Do you remember how we used to stalk Roger on the train home after school?"
"Yes! He'd sit in the same carriage, looking hip and handsome, with that smirk on his face."
"Oh yes! I dreamt of him smirking at me all through year 10."
"All the girls did. He's still in good shape."

Emily sighed. "Just what I need, an intellect free zone with a hot bod."

"You're starting to sound like me, Emms."

"Well, it's been a while."

"How long?"

Emily thought. "Two years?"

"You've only been divorced for six months."

"We lost contact way before then."

Sue stood. "I'm tired. Do you mind if we head back home?"

Emily looped her arm around Sue, without speaking. As they walked, joggers passed them on the narrow track.

"It's lovely here," Sue spoke, "to think I've never been to this park. On a day like this, I believe anything is possible. Maybe I could work for an NGO, after all."

"Maybe I'll re-train as an astronaut and give Bob the one finger salute from space."

Sue laughed and held Emily's arm tightly. "If I change gears and slow down, what was it all for in the end? It seems like I was running away from the thing I loved most."

Emily didn't reply, just held her arm as they walked on. Moist earth beneath their feet, they walked back to the carpark in silence.

Chapter 29

"C'mon, Mimi" Emily tugged at the leash, "let's bring the croissants to Sylvia."

She walked up the garden path, Mimi bounding ahead. The outdoor table was set with plates and tea cups and she knocked on the front door. Her knock sounded hollow and Emily fought an uneasy feeling as she knocked again.

"Hello?" She pushed the front door open and peered down the hallway. "Sylvia?" Mimi pushed past her and bounded down to the kitchen.

She followed behind as she heard Mimi whimpering.

"Oh Sylvia!" She saw a slight shape on the kitchen floor and ran to her.

"How silly am I, my girl?" Sylvia shook her head. "I slipped on a wet patch on the floor just now. Didn't know where I was for a few minutes."

"Can you feel your toes? Your arms?"

Sylvia looked at her. "Do you think I'm an idiot?" She gingerly swung to her side and put an arm on the floor. "I can do this myself, if you'd rather."

"Maybe I should call an ambulance, to have you checked before we move you."

"That's not going to happen." Sylvia reached for the kitchen chair and slowly pulled herself to her knees.

"Has this happened before?"

"Damn pipes leak under the sink. It floods the floor occasionally."

"Have a plumber fix it. For goodness sake, Sylvia, for a sensible woman, you can be remarkably silly sometimes."

Emily helped Sylvia stand. She stood, holding the chair for a moment, then sank into it and closed her eyes. A tremor ran the length of her arm and she tried to steady the movement.

Mimi placed her head on Sylvia's lap and a gentle pat was her reward.

"Please don't call a plumber." Sylvia spoke. "He'll report me to DOCS and they'll send someone to assess my home and next thing you know, I'll be in a retirement village and Mimi will be gone. No, thank you." She eyed her. "Don't you go saying anything."

"I'll call my plumber and ask him to inspect it with me. I'll tell him you're my aunt. He's not the brightest spark, so you're safe from the government for now."

"I wasn't raised to lie."

"If you want to keep living in your home, drop your standards."

"Oh you laugh at me but people talk. Kids are the worst, they dob their parents in to get their inheritance. I've seen it happen."

"Well, we're not related, so you have no problems there. The only thing I could take from you is Mimi and I don't want her, thanks very much." She eyed her. "How's your hip feel?"

Sylvia stood and took a step. "Perfect. Aren't I lucky, Mims?" She patted the dog. "Did you bring me croissants?"

"If you mean me, yes I did." Emily remarked drily.

Sylvia laughed. "Dependency makes me ungracious." She stepped forward gingerly. "No damage done. Be a dear and wipe the floor for me, please, I don't want to take another tumble. You'll have to re-brew the kettle while you're at it, the tea's stood too long, it'll be bitter now."

Emily watched Sylvia from the corner of her eye as she sat at the table. Her arms rested on the chair, liver spots and deep veins criss-crossed them. Her frailty smote Emily's heart.

"Where are your rags?"

"Under the sink." Sylvia was barely audible.

She peered underneath. "The leak seems to have stopped for now. You should leave some rags out to prevent yourself from tumbling again." She grinned. "Who's bossy now?"

"My middle aged knight in shining armour has saved me again. This could be a full time job

"Don't know how to save myself." She filled the kettle. "Let's sit inside today, that was a bad tumble."

"Absolutely not, there's a day out there to be lived." Sylvia moved across to her broom cupboard. "I'll need this." She held a walking stick at length and Emily noticed her down-turned mouth.

"Of course. Mims, you lead the way. I'll follow behind you, Sylvia."

"There's no need." She made no further protest and Emily watched her slow progress up the hallway. At the doorway, Sylvia leaned heavily on the cane.

They reached the porch and Sylvia threw the stick on the floor. "It's not a long journey," she spoke, "from childhood to old age. Do you remember as a girl, thinking you would be young and strong forever? Dancing with your fella at night, dreaming of the good years to come. Bending down to plant a seed, knowing you had years to watch it grow to maturity?" She gazed out at her garden. "Those infinite years pass, till all you have left is memories and a piece of wood to propel your old self onwards."

She sat in silence as Emily poured tea.

"You do really well, Sylvia. Some women in their seventies don't get about like you."

"But I'm exceptional." They grinned at each other. "You'll never believe these old legs loved to ski."

"Really?"

"I was mad for it, just as good on a set of skis as I was in the saddle. John Edward said that was the only thing he'd ask me to give up, said I skied down a mountain like a woman possessed." She laughed. "So I did, but I had tremendous balance. My Poppy taught me to be still in the eye of any storm."

"Did you really give up because of your husband?"

"Of course, we'd only just married. He wanted me to stop all strenuous sport, to give my body a rest. He loved me so much, just imagine." She lifted her tea cup. "After a while, I got used to it. It felt unseemly to gallivant around on a horse when we went back to Adaminaby. I guess you change when you take on responsibilities."

Emily stared at her face. Reminiscence transformed her features. A girlish gleam in her eyes warmed her skin, it was translucent with love.

"Did you miss it?"

"Not while I had John Edward. I was an accountant's wife and I wanted him to be proud of me." She drained her cup. "When I lost him, I felt the loss of my athletic life keenly. It was thirty years since I'd ridden and I knew my hip wouldn't hold up in a saddle again. Isn't that funny, to mourn something after so long? I gave myself a good talking to, let me tell you." She waited for Emily to refill her cup. "I was blessed to have it when I was young. Blessed to have this great age too. Mother always said to count the sunny side of life, not moan about the losses."

"Did you give up riding to help you conceive?"

Sylvia started.

"Sorry, that's none of my business."

"There's another wretched apology. You've been doing so well lately, too." Sylvia nodded. "You can ask me anything. Yes, that's right. It's not like today, women have more choices to help them conceive. We had next to nothing, so I had to accept my fate."

"Do you think you would've tried IVF?"

"Lord, yes. John Edward loved science, he would have been an expert on it. It was just getting media coverage when he was ill, test tube babies and all that. We talked about how exciting an advance it was."

"Your church didn't like it."

"Bugger the church, they didn't understand married life at all. Look at all the loonies they unleashed on precious children. I'll get myself excommunicated if I'm not careful." She broke a croissant and fed Mimi a piece absent-mindedly. "You said you weren't a religious woman."

Emily shook her head. "Mum was raised Catholic but she stopped practising her faith when we were little. She said her church didn't help us when we really needed it."

Emily pulled an envelope from her pocket. "I have something for you." She placed it on Sylvia's lap.

"What on earth?"
Sylvia opened the envelope and peered through her glasses at the tickets inside. She placed the envelope on the table and sat in silence. "Don't overwhelm me all at once." Emily murmured.
"My girl, it's not that I'm ungrateful." Sylvia glanced at her. "I'm just too old. And it's too late at night."
"It's a matinee. I'll drive you to the steps of the Opera House and you can take the rehearsal lift direct to the theatre. I already enquired." Emily leaned forward. "Please Sylvia, I don't have an Opera buddy. My girlfriend hates it and my kids wouldn't be seen dead there. You'll leave me out of pocket and companion-less." She smiled. "I'm racking my brain for more blackmail but I think I've exhausted myself. No wait, its 'La Boheme', our favourite."

"Yes," Sylvia stopped her. "Thank you, I'll go. I said I'd never go again but I'll make an exception for you."
"I'm honoured." Emily smiled. "It's two weeks from Saturday, so dust off your glad rags."
"You're good to me." Sylvia stood stiffly. I don't believe you've had the love you deserve in your life. A good man would make you blossom." She motioned to the walking stick and Emily lifted it for her. "I need to lie down, with all the excitement today. Would you be a love and carry the tray into the kitchen." As she passed Emily, Sylvia gave her arm a squeeze. "Thank you," she spoke softly.
Emily watched her halting walk inside the house.

…................................

Emily stood at the chalkboard and wrote:
"Past and present, so intimately intertwined. Do we ever say goodbye to the past whilst memory survives?"

Chapter 30

"Wow, the only time I've seen you head-first in a toilet bowl is after a big night out."

Sue wiped her mouth and sat slumped on the bathroom floor.

"Don't flush it, Emms. I'll do it."

"Habit. I've had kids, remember?" She crouched beside her. "How long have you been doing this?"

"About a day after I stopped the anti-nausea medication."

"Because you obviously didn't need it."

Sue nodded.

"Where is it?"

"Kitchen cupboard above the stove."

"Wait here."

"I'm not going anywhere."

Emily returned, packet in hand, to find Sue over the bowl again. "Oh dear."

"Oh fuck, more like it." Sue sat up. "How did I end up here?"

"Is that an existential question or a rhetorical one?"

"Rhetorical."

"Good, then I don't need to answer." She held up a glass and a tablet. "Open wide."

Sue silently accepted the medication. "I hate being full of drugs. God knows what they're doing to my body."

"The alternative isn't particularly attractive."

"You should have been this ballsy with Bob. He'd have liked it."

"I didn't love him, remember? You, I do."

Sue squeezed her hand. "I need to hear that today."

Emily peered into the toilet bowl. "That's an interesting colour vomit. From a mum's perspective, it's really something."

Sue closed her eyes. "I don't think the nausea medication kicks in straight away. We could be here awhile."

"Here, sit on a cushion." Emily held it out. "I took one for me too."

"You'll stay?"

"Of course."

"Thanks." Sue kept her eyes closed and Emily noticed the pallor of her skin.

"True or false." Sue opened her eyes. "I look like a corpse today."

"True."

"There's a strange odour coming from my pores."

Emily hesitated.

"True or false. You know the rules."

"True."

Sue grimaced. "Regardless of these factors, if the new office courier saw me today, he'd ask me out."

"False."

"Your honesty nowadays is disturbing."

"The divorce factor. Strips away the bullshit."

"Your turn."

"Sue, we haven't played this game in years."

"I need it today. By the by, when we got kicked out of science for playing this in year 10, it was your fault."

"Obviously anti nausea and memory loss tablets combined." Emily shifted her cushion. "It's no good, you can't get comfortable on tiles."

"Your turn."

Emily smiled. "You are like a sister to me."

"True."

"You will recover fully and banter with me until we are old ladies sitting on a park bench."

"True."

"The courier would rather ask me out, he has a thing for menopausal women."

"False." Sue held her stomach and Emily slid further sideways.

"Just in case you projectile vomit."

Sue nodded. "My turn." She closed her eyes again. "You

have been holding back on me over the years about your father."

Emily was silent and Sue opened her eyes. "Waiting."

"True."

"He was an associate of Robert Trimbole and murdered a couple of people."

Emily laughed. "False, at least to the best of my knowledge."

"He hurt you badly over the years. And your mother. And your mysterious brother."

Emily whispered. "True."

They stared at each other. Sue went to speak but Emily held up her hand. "You've asked three questions. My turn again."

"I could never cheat with you."

"That's why we got kicked out of science class." Emily looked down as she spoke. "At a New Year's Eve party at our place, when the kids were small, Bob made a pass at you."

"True."

"You told him to piss off."

"True."

"That's when he started calling you the bitch."

"The bastard. True, I mean."

They smiled wryly at each other.

Sue leaned over the bowl. "Just give me a minute."

Emily rubbed her back as she retched again. "Here's a glass of water."

"Thanks. Nothing like the taste of vomit in your mouth. I'm amazed someone's not thought of it as a appetite suppressant. Make a fortune." Sue sat again. "My turn."

"Let's stop, it might be upsetting you."

"It's getting me through the moment." Sue placed the glass beside her with an unsteady hand.

"Your father beat you once." She looked directly at Emily. "In year 8."

"I fell over."

"True or false, Emms."

Emily stood. "This is a childish game."

Sue caught her hand. "Stay with me. If I can vomit multicoloured spray in front of you, you can be honest with me. True or false?"

"True."

"The bastard. I knew it."

"It was just the once. I was smart to him and he lashed out. He was mortified afterwards."

"He hit your mother."

"You're turning a fun game we played as teenagers into an interrogation."

"That's not true." Sue looked at her. "I always wanted to ask you but you pushed me away. There were moments when I thought I could approach you but you became dismissive and distant." She raised her hands in the air. "If I can't ask you now, when I'm fighting for my life, when will we be honest with each other?" She broke off with a sob. "It's just a question, Emms. It won't define how I see you."

"True." Emily spoke in a low voice. "He hit her many times, mostly in front of Rodney and me."

Sue closed her eyes again. "You hated him."

"True. With all of my heart. Still do." Emily stood. "There, you got your three questions. I have to go. Will you be OK now?"

"I don't think I have anything left to bring up." Sue looked up as she replied but Emily had gone. She heard the front door open and then the sound of it closing softly.

Chapter 31

"Oh la la, Sylvia! You look gorgeous."

"You're being absurd, my girl. I look like an old woman about to topple over. But I'm glad you like my dress, John Edward bought it for my sixtieth."

"More power to you that you still fit into it."

"I would never let myself go to fat." Sylvia tucked her legs into the car.

Emily manoeuvred onto the road from the driveway. "I've left us two hours to spare. We can have a leisurely lunch first."

Sylvia nodded but Emily saw the excited gleam in her eye. "There's life in you yet." She thought.

"When did you first see La Boheme?"

"At La Scala in Milan. We went on a tour with our church. One of the girls, Marissa, was a trained singer, so she organised the tickets. After that, we were hooked. My husband had a marvellous baritone, he led the choir for years. I can barely squeak out a tune, so I really admire singers." Sylvia looked out the window. "It's quite luxurious to sit in a car again." She inspected the interior. "You're very neat. Same at home?"

"Obsessively so. That's why I've been given a slothful son, his yin balances my yang."

"Was your husband tidy?"

"He was never home long enough for me to find out."

"I see."

"Did you get your license?"

"Yes, but I used it very little. I sold the car after I was widowed."

"I'd have thought with your love of speed, a car would have been the ultimate toy."

"Not compared to a horse. That's equal parts showmanship and skill. Trapped in a large piece of metal, strapped into a seat belt, doesn't compare."

"Tell that to Jack Brabham."

They were silent as Emily approached the city. She negotiated the turn onto Macquarie Street and Sylvia leaned forward as the white sails of the Opera House came into view.

"Never loses its magic."

"I'll drop you at the stairs, then go park the car. I'll meet you inside."

"No, I'll come with you."

"It's a long walk, Sylvia."

"I insist."

Emily remained silent. She parked the car and lifted the walking stick from the back seat.

"I'll manage without it."

"Sylvia, stop being so stubborn. No one will care."

"But I do." Sylvia smoothed her dress and patted her hair as she walked beside Emily, who held the walking stick in her hand.

"That thing ages you, Emily. You should've left it in the car."

Emily rolled her eyes as they walked slowly to the forecourt.

"Just ask if you need it."

"I think you're going deaf. I've made it plain how I feel."

Emily's stress levels rose at their slow progress. "I should have given us three hours, not two." She thought.

"You're fretting, my girl. You need to stop clenching your hands and relax. How can I enjoy myself if I have you fussing over me like a mother hen?"

"I'll kill her." Emily thought.

"Let's eat cake." Sylvia paused at the forecourt. "I'll take the lift you mentioned."

"Of course, I'll speak to the staff." As Emily walked away, she looked down at her hands. "She's right, canny old bird."

Sylvia looked up as Emily approached with a staff member.

"This way, ma'am." The young woman held out a wheelchair. "We ask you to use this in the lift, for safety reasons."

"Just for the lift." Sylvia waved a finger at her. "If I see anyone I know, I'll push you into it." Sylvia looked at the girl with her keen eyes.

"Yes, ma'am. My grandmother would do the same thing." She smiled at her.

"Completely charmed by her." Emily mused to herself. She followed behind them.

Sylvia's bright eyes darted about. "Just as I remembered it!"

"Did you come here often, ma'am?"

"Every winter season with my husband. We were patrons since the opening in the seventies."

"He's not with you now, ma'am?"

"I lost him nearly thirty years ago."

"I'm sorry to hear that." She leaned over to Sylvia. "I've taken you close to the cafe but it's private here, so no one will see you leave the chair." She turned to Emily. "Call me if you need it on the way down. It's been a pleasure meeting you, ma'am."

Sylvia squeezed her hand. "You've been delightful."

The young woman beamed as she left them.

"You could charm sparrows from trees." Emily spoke. "Not with me, though."

"You won't listen to me, my girl. You just smother me with your good intentions." She clutched Emily's arm. "I want cake and a good glass of champagne."

"That hardly constitutes lunch."

"It does at my age." Sylvia paused for breath. "Now, don't lecture me. The walk took more out of me than I thought. After that admission, I imagine you'd like to crack that walking stick over my head."

Emily shook her head. "Too many witnesses. Maybe on the way down in the lift." She held onto Sylvia as they entered the cafe.

....

Sylvia scooped a mouthful of ice cream into her mouth. "I love bread and butter pudding."

Emily was silent.

"You find me rude."

"Sometimes."

"But you're too eager to please. That must've driven your husband insane. Men like spirit in a woman."

"You're making assumptions about me. We aren't all blessed with faithful husbands."

"I see, he was a scoundrel. You should have left him and taken the children."

"You didn't have a family, so you don't know what it's like. The thought of pulling them out of school, changing areas, weekend custody. Some of us just sit it out, till we're so dead in spirit, there's nothing left of us."

Sylvia was silent.

"I'm sorry, that was rude."

"No, you're right, I didn't have a family, just a series of dogs. I don't know."

They sat in silence.

Sylvia pointed her spoon at Emily's dessert. "You should finish your dessert. It's delicious."

"You ordered it for me. And I always lose my appetite in a quarrel."

"We're not quarrelling. You told me to mind my own business, as good as. No offence taken."

Sylvia eyed Emily. "You're too sensitive, you need to toughen up. You won't live long with that soft exterior, people will trounce on you. Probably already have."

Emily pushed her plate across. "Here, you finish it. I've barely touched it."

"Thank you, I will." Sylvia's eyes sparkled, a mix of champagne and sugar.

"Sylvia!"

They glanced up in the direction of the voice.

"Oh no!" Sylvia murmured. "Please God, not her."

A tall, white haired woman approached them. She leaned on the arm of an equally tall, young man.

"Sylvia Baker, I knew it was you!"

"Dulcie, it's been a long time." Sylvia stood and they embraced. The woman swamped Sylvia in height.

"Too long." Dulcie stood back and eyed her. "Still thin as a whippet." She eyed Emily.

"This is my neighbour, Emily. This is Dulcie, we were in the Catholic Women's League together."

Dulcie laughed. "We never did anything but bake scones together for the local soup kitchen. Still, we feed a few, I guess that counts."

"Indeed. Is this your grandson?"

"Yes, Marie's youngest. Charlie takes Nan to the Opera every Winter."

"What a fine boy." Sylvia clutched the table. "I'll let you both peruse the menu. Bread and butter pudding is as good as it was back in the day."

"Call me this week, Sylvia. My number's the same. We'll have a catch up yarn. I'd love to know your news. I've haven't heard anything since John..."

"I know." Sylvia sat abruptly and turned away. "Good to see you, Dulcie. Enjoy the show."

Emily watched as they walked away.

"What a day of shocks!" Sylvia muttered. "There's a face I thought I'd never see again." She watched as they joined the queue at the cafe.

"You're grieving too," Emily mused, "but we're silent to each other's pain." She glanced at her watch.

"We should head up." She spoke, "the show will begin in half and hour. Best if we have plenty of time to get there."

Sylvia pushed the plate away and nodded. "Let's."

They stood and Sylvia leaned on Emily. She motioned to the walking stick and Emily handed it to her.

"Thank you."

Chapter 32 - View 3

"The mornings are getting fresh." Emily jumped up and down on the spot. "If only I could get Mimi to move faster. This stopping and sniffing business is killing me."

"Classic dog behaviour." Stan smiled. "How's your sick friend?"

"Which one, the young, cantankerous one or the old, cantankerous one?

"Either or."

"Both taxing my sanity." She glanced at her watch. "This is a late morning for you, you're usually gone by now."

"I don't see Alice every day now. I go every second day and I really look forward to the off day. Her eyes don't light up when she sees me anymore. I feel she's way beyond me now, beyond my prayers."

Emily squeezed his arm. "If you need a dog walker for a complete day of rest, I'm your man. So to speak."

They walked on in the windy park. The dogs broke into a run up the hill and they followed behind.

"Hello."

Emily turned at the voice and winced. "Oh no!"

"Who's that?"

"You have to help me."

A short man strode towards them, his stocky frame bulging out of his track pants and windcheater. A dainty whippet kept pace with him.

"Good morning! I saw you from my bedroom window." He held out his hand to Stan. "Gerald. I bought the blue painted terrace across the road there."

"Stan."

Gerald nodded at Emily. "We met yesterday. I told her I was new and she said you're a friendly mob here."

Stan was silent.

"Brittany just needs a quick sprint around the park, there's not much of her to exercise."

Emily managed a smile.

"Heading for coffee? I'll join you." He took Emily's elbow as he walked alongside them.

She looked at Stan in desperation. "You'll join us?"

"Umm.."

She grabbed his arm. "Great, let's go."

"Where've you moved from?" Stan roused himself to speak.

"Potts Point. I lived in a three bedder after I separated from my wife. Never settled there, more down to earth here. Bugger a cup of sugar for a new neighbour, they wouldn't even offer a smile. I saw a couple of them cross the road to avoid me. Can you believe it?"

Stan's eyes twinkled at Emily.

Gerald's eyes darted between them. "What's your trade, Stan?"

"Retired sparkie."

"I could use you to fix up a couple of old wires. Thought I'd electrocute myself when I switched a lamp on last night."

"I'll recommend someone to you."

"Suit yourself. I pay well."

Mimi whined and Emily bent to her. "Let's get you a croissant."

Gerald held her elbow again. "My shout. Not a bad way to start the morning, hey?" He looked between the two of them. "Not treading on any toes, am I?"

They both shook their heads.

"I like my neighbours already." Gerald spoke to Brittany as he led the way.

They crossed the road to the cafe and Gerard motioned to a table. "I'll get coffees."

"I'll have...."

"No good, he's gone." said Emily. "God give me patience."

"You'll need more than that. Will we be allowed to hold our own cups?"

"I'm not sure."

Gerald bustled back to the table.

"I ordered caramel slices all round." He sat down. "Potts Point prices. Not that I'm complaining. It's a lot for frothed milk and a shot of caffeine."

Brittany whined and Gerald pushed her away with his shoe. "She's Caroline's dog, my ex wife. She's at Noosa now, recovering from her latest bout of plastic surgery. It's plastic surgeons that are doing well at the moment. That and my line."

"What do you do?"

"Egg production. My company services metropolitan Sydney. We have two supermarket chains. People don't stop buying eggs in a recession."

"Keep you out of trouble." Stan drained his cup, his eyes twinkling again at Emily. "I'll see you tomorrow. Good to meet you, Gerald." Stan untethered Ralf and walked away quickly. He winked at Emily as he escaped.

"A bit sensitive."

"Stan's under a lot of stress."

"I've seen it before. Men intimidated by another's success." Gerald leaned back in his chair. "What's your story?"

"Pardon?"

"Single, divorced, de facto?"

"Just divorced, two kids. One's just moved back in."

"Boomerangs. Got no time for them. No one took me in when things got tough."

"My son's great."

"I can't tell you what to do."

"But you want to." Emily thought.

"Are you retired?"

"I work part-time. Building up my super."

"I've got a financial adviser you can go to. A good bloke. I'll call him and arrange a meeting. We'll do a day trip to Palm Beach."

"No thanks."

"Independent spirit, I like that."

Emily looked down at her lap. She noticed her hands were trembling. She sat on them.

"God, get me out of here." She prayed.

"If you aren't eating your caramel slice, I will." He reached over and she snatched the plate away.

"Mimi eats all my left overs." Emily held Mimi's lead and stood abruptly. "I have to go."

"You have sexy eyes." Gerald appraised her as she stood before him. "You won't be single long. Some guy will snap you up."

"Keep eating Mulvey eggs!" He called out as she hurried out the front entrance.

…......................

Back in her flat, she glanced at her watch. "Shit, I'll be late for work." She twirled the chalk in her hands, then wrote in a jerky hand: "Morons inhabit too much space on this planet. I gain a new, unwanted view of me: sexy eyes. Enough said."

Chapter 33

"Sar, you take the bedroom. I'll sleep on the couch."

"I'm not sleeping in your sweat box, Dom." Sarah sat upright on the sofa. "I'll sleep here. Is that alright, Mum?"

"Do you want to call Matt, let him know you've arrived safe?"

She shook her head and lay down.

"I'm heading to bed. Night all."

"Night, son."

Emily began to rub Sarah's feet. "Long drive you've had."

"Yes."

"Are you tired?"

"No."

"Hungry?"

"No."

Emily bit her lip.

"Don't do that, Mum. Makes you look like you're sucking in dentures. Matt's grandma does it, totally gross."

"Thanks for the tip. How's the new school going?"

"Excellent."

"And the house?"

"Brilliant."

"Give me something, Sarah. I'm nearly at the end of twenty questions."

"I'm just visiting."

"At 11pm on a Friday night? Don't get me wrong, I'm thrilled you're here but..."

"Got any tea?"

Sarah jumped up and walked across to the kitchen. She read the chalk board. "Eww! Who was the creep that said that?"

Emily shrugged. "Don't go there."

Sarah filled the kettle. "Does this feel like home yet?"

"Some days, yes. When you're both here."

"When's Dom leaving?" Sarah dunked a tea bag into her mug. "If

Matt and I broke up, I wouldn't move in with you."

"Something's up?"

"No. A couple of his Sydney mates are over for the weekend to catch up. I didn't want to come between pizza, beer and the football. We're good with space." She sat back on the sofa. "It's cosy here. Picture update?"

"I'm still watching where light falls on the walls."

"Take all of a day." Sarah sipped her tea. "Dom's like you, he watches where he places every step. I couldn't live that way."

"I don't think you know Dom that well. He doesn't want the traditional road of marriage and kids."

"Doesn't want the responsibility more like it. Jenny was probably pressuring him to seal the deal with a ring and he baulked."

"He still loves her. I didn't realise how much."

Sarah walked over to the fridge and peered inside. "God, I'm ravenous." She leaned her head on the door. "I'm so tired now."

"Sit, honey, I'll make you a sandwich."

"Don't fuss! You're always trying to fix things for us."

She opened the fridge again and took out a loaf of bread and jerked the cutlery drawer open. "See, I'm not like Dom, I won't play the sympathy card." She rummaged the drawer and tossed cutlery out as she searched. "Every bloody gizmo in here but a knife."

"Second drawer."

Sarah held a finger to her lips. "Shh Mum, hear that noise? It's like a cracking sound." She walked onto the balcony and peered over the railing. "Your fountain's leaking."

"What, again?"

"Shooting water everywhere."

Emily raced over and looked down. "Oh my God! There's three of us here, the Committee will think I'm running my own gang." She turned to Sarah. "Do you have a camera? We have to take a photo to prove it wasn't us."

Sarah laughed. "Why would they think that? Who are these people you live with?"

"We're each other's alibi. No one can pin it on me."

"Mum," Sarah shook her shoulders, "you're not making any sense."

Emily stared at the fountain, transfixed.

"Do you know where the water main is? We'll have to turn it off or the front lawn will flood."

"Don't go down there! I'll get arrested."

"Oh, for God's sake! Where's the mains box?"

"In the far corner." Emily stood at the railing. "Wear something dark. Do you have a hoodie?"

Sarah swore under her breath. "Where's the torch? Never mind, I remember." She marched to the front door and Emily waited for her. She watched as Sarah squelched her way past the statue.

"Ouch!"

"Careful, darling. What did you step on?"

Sarah shone the torch on the ground. "Someone's chopped its head off."

"Don't touch it, you'll leave fingerprints."

"Eww, disgusting. They hacked its willy off too."

"That's some sick mind at work."

Sarah waddled across the grass and opened the mains box. A light shone from the other side of the lawn.

Rhonda's chins appeared under torchlight. "Who's there?" She shone her torch at Sarah.

Sarah dropped her torch in shock.

The triple chins advanced.

"Rhonda, don't be silly. Sarah's my daughter."

Rhonda glanced up sharply as Emily called out from above.

"Another member of your family at the scene of the crime."

"She's turning off the water, if you must know."

"Why didn't you go down with her?"

Sarah interrupted. "Mum's paranoid she'll get the blame."

"Well, why not? I usually cop all of the suspicion. Good to share it around."

Sarah held her hand out. "I'm Sarah. I think I turned the right gauge off."

They stared at the fountain as the spurts slowed into drips.

"Very sensible of you."

"One person in my family has to be." Sarah shrugged. "Does this happen often?"

"Yes, bloody thing's costing us a fortune. I'm going to write a letter of complaint to the Strata Manager. I'm sick of humouring some stuck up, pretentious North Shore bitch. She can move back to Neutral Bay, as far as I'm concerned. She and all her wanker buddies can fill their courtyards with mouldy bits of marble and pretend they're so cultured. She just has to bat those faded eyes at Gus and he falls for it all over again. Ugh!" Rhonda squelched past Sarah and examined the fountain. "I'd love to take a hammer to it and finish it off." She glanced at Sarah. "Good job with the water. I'll let you back in."

"Thanks." Sarah took off her shoes and wrung her socks.

"Thanks, darling."

"Why are you so down on your neighbours? Rhonda's good value."

Emily smiled. "Take charge women always get on with each other. She senses my incompetence."

Sarah slipped her jeans off. "I've got to shower, I'm dripping on your rug." She stood still, shivering.

The dark circles under her eyes were startling against her beautiful skin. "I can't get pregnant. We've tried for three months but it won't happen. It's probably me. Poor Matt."

Emily led her to the sofa.

"Mum, I'm soaking."

"Take the throw rug."

"I dread it now, the waiting time between my period. It's like a monthly report of my body's failure to do something natural."

"If you stop worrying about it, it will happen naturally."

"How long did it take you?"

"Sarah, that's a silly comparison."

"How long?"

"Within a couple of months but ..."

"It's me." Sarah folded her legs underneath her. "It won't happen, I know it."

"Honey, you're just so intense. That could be hindering your body's natural rhythm."

"Maybe I don't want to be pregnant."

Emily stared at her.

"I remember in art class at high school, we learnt about light and shade. I was bored out of my brains at the time but I can't stop thinking about it now. It's just Matt and I in Gosford, we don't have our network of friends to bring light and shade to our relationship. I stare at him across the dinner table and wonder, is this all my life will be? Trying to get pregnant to a man I'm not sure of anymore. How did this happen in the space of two months? Was I always lying to myself?"

She brushed her eyes. "Don't tell Dom, he'll laugh at me. I'm not like him, I don't want to throw Matt away, I'm just not sure of me anymore. It feels so weird, because I don't suffer self doubt. I always know what I want." She ran a nervy hand over the leather. "Being on our own up there, I just feel lonely, especially when we're together. I can't shake the feeling." She stood abruptly. "I'm taking a shower."

Emily walked onto the balcony as she waited for her. The street was in complete silence. Sylvia's house was in darkness and she watched the kitchen curtain billow in the slow wind.

She turned as Sarah re-entered the room.

"I'll pour some aspirin in a glass of water for you."

"Thanks."

Sarah lay on a pillow on the sofa and tucked herself into a blanket.

"I'll watch some TV with you." She channel surfed and set the volume on low.

Emily watched as Sarah's eyes closed and her limbs relaxed. Her blonde hair streaked across the pillow.

Emily gently lifted the strands away from her face, folding them behind her neck.

Somewhere within her, a lullaby arose in her mind. She sang the words in a whisper to her sleeping daughter, her throat catching on the lyrics.

Chapter 34

"You look feral."

"Shut up!"

"Woa, go Emily." Serena perched on her desk and pulled her skirt downwards. "I turned thirty last week. It's getting harder to pour myself into these clothes." She cocked her head to one side. "Want to talk about it?"

Emily shook her head.

Silence.

"Maybe just a little bit."

"I thought so."

Emily rested her head on her hands. "I'm surrounded by stupid men." She spoke softly.

"Not Dominic."

Emily laughed. "Not my son. Old, stupid men who try to think for me."

Serena was silent and Emily glanced up, to see her brush her eyes.

"Are you alright? I didn't mean to upset you."

"I don't want to be like you in twenty years time. I'm tired of stupid men now, what'll I be like then?"

Emily gripped her hand. "Make better choices than me, that's what. Don't settle for comfort, seek a kindred spirit who makes your heart happy."

Serena bent her head so low, her curls covered her face.

"Just like Dom." Emily thought.

"I thought my last boyfriend was the one, we were together for four years. But it ended. I would've worked at it, like my mum and dad did. My dad was a hero, he stuck it through when Mum got sick. Men like that don't exist anymore."

Emily squeezed her hand. "They do and you know it. Don't settle for ordinary, you're too extraordinary for that."

"Thanks." Serena held her hand to her cheeks. "I go all rosy when I cry." She straightened her shoulders. "It's not like I need a man, I have a great career and life." She played with the stapler as she spoke. "But when I see couples walk together, caught up in a small world of their own, I envy them. I want that moment with a great guy on my arm, committed to me and all that life can throw at us."

"Look for that extraordinary man. You're worth it."

"Someone like Dominic?"

Emily hesitated.

"Not worth your precious son, right?" Serena stood and walked away.

"Serena" Emily called out but she continued walking.

Chapter 35- Round 4

Gus cleared his throat. "I've got the police report." He handed out photocopies. "We'll need to send letters out to all owners."

Cecilia and Rhonda stood apart from each other as he continued. "The police don't believe its neighbourhood kids." He leaned forward and whispered. "They think it's someone with a vendetta."

Flossie's needles clattered and she held them firmly in her gnarled hands. "Shocking," she murmured, "just shocking."

Gus continued. "If we repair it.."

"If?" Cecilia interjected.

He spoke over her. "I don't think we should re-install it, it's been decapitated and emasculated. I think the poor little bastard deserves a peaceful retirement on your balcony."

Cecilia stamped her foot. "Give into an act of terrorism?"

Emily smiled.

Cecilia stared at her.

"Choice of words." Emily muttered.

Rhonda spoke. "You're always silent on this topic."

"I'm quiet natured."

"We need go getters on this committee. Not wishy washy members who don't say boo."

Gus held up a hand. "Rhonda, whoever's doing this will love it if we turn on each other. Let's not let them win."

"Here, here!" Cecilia clapped her hands. "And for that reason we must re-install it. I've taken the cherub to Luigi, who'll repair it at cost price. He said he's not seen such savagery since the war and we should press charges."

"If we catch them." Rhonda replied. "Even Emily hasn't seen them and she lives directly above. She's had drunken friends catch glimpses, apparently."

Flossie finished a row, then looked up. "Can your friends give police a description?"

"Big and furry." Rhonda interjected. "Apparently."

Gus looked at Emily. "Did you see anything this time?"
"No," she shifted on the fence. "My daughter heard the snap."
"I insist we give it a year." Cecilia spoke.
"No matter the cost?" Rhonda replied.
"If someone stopped vandalising it, there'd be no cost." Cecilia continued. "We're not giving into someone bully without a life. It's these loonies that run the world and cause no end of problems for the rest of us." She thrust a small piece of marble into Rhonda's hand. "Look at it, it's ruined!"
Rhonda's eyes widened. "Is this the peni..."
"Yes, the spout." Cecilia laughed, "no good giving it to you, you probably haven't held one for years." She snatched it back. "Gus would have more use for it."
Emily watched as the Gus's ear lobes went bright red.
"Honestly," Cecilia held his arm, "we've known for ages you're gay."
Flossie dropped a needle and Gus bent to retrieve it.
"If you left your knitting at home, you could actually contribute to the discussions." Cecilia spoke.
"You girls fight so much, I need something to settle my nerves."
Flossie nodded at Emily. "Not you, nice quiet little thing you are."

Emily cleared her throat. "We could re-position the statue, move it to the back garden. There's a lovely patch of lawn out there. It would look nice and there'd be less chance of a break in or vandalism because the area's floodlit at night."
"Absolutely no chance." Cecilia turned on her. "It was to be the focal point of the front lawn. I'm not shunting it out the back, that's admitting defeat."
"What a stupid idea." Rhonda joined in. "We'd still have to foot the repair bill for that pathetic lump of marble."
Emily bit her lip.
"How much have we spent already?" Rhonda glanced at Gus.

"About fifteen hundred."

"Oh my God! I could go around the world on that."

"Why don't you?" muttered Cecilia.

"Ladies," interjected Gus. "Why don't we set up a cost cap? We stop repairs after two thousand dollars."

"We're just asking for someone to do it again." Cecilia sighed.

"It's beyond generosity." Rhonda interjected. "And sanity."

"I know it will happen again." Cecilia spoke.

"Then save us another five hundred dollars and donate that monstrosity to Luigi. He can attach it to some wog's tombstone." Rhonda stood. "I'm done with this." She left them without another word.

Cecilia moved towards Gus. "You know how I feel about her." She fluttered her eyes at him. "We should vote her off the committee. She's just a giant ball of vile, really she is."

Emily stood and quietly said goodnight. No one turned to acknowledge her.

Flossie watched her leave. "Nice lass."

Cecilia frowned. "You think? There's something about her I don't like. She's too sly for my taste."

…......................

Emily opened her front door.

"You ok, mum?" Dominic looked up from the sofa.

She strode across to the chalk board and lifted a piece of chalk. "Negotiating with jerks," she wrote, "is like offering Hitler classes in humility."

"That bad, huh?" Dominic looked across. "Did Rhonda ask after me?"

Emily leaned on the kitchen benchtop. "Say something that will remind me that people are good and wise."

"That's a tall order, Mum."

"No need, son," she smiled at him, "I'm feeling better already."

Chapter 36

"God, you drive like a freakin' grandmother!"

Emily sighed as she stopped at the roundabout.

"It's a sixty zone and you're doing forty. Is it for my benefit?"

"I don't want you to get car sick."

"Stop thinking for me."

Emily turned into Sue's street. "Home safe."

"I could have jogged from the clinic and gotten home before you."
Sue snapped her seat belt open and opened the car door. "Thank God
that was my last chemo session."

"Amen to that. Don't forget to take your anti nausea meds."

"I'm going to put a salsa CD on and shake my middle aged
butt to celebrate. See ya." Sue slammed the car door.

Emily sat still and closed her eyes.

The car door opened again. "I'm a bitch, aren't I? I've criticised you
all afternoon and you haven't said a word."

Emily nodded.

"You must hate me." Sue paused. "Emms, I don't want to go inside."

"Then get back in the car and we'll go for a drive to Manly. We'll eat
ice cream and chase seagulls on the beach."

"Different to thirty years ago. We chased boys then."

"Seagulls are easier to catch at our age."

"True." Sue reclined her seat. "Do you mind if I nap?"

"Don't snore." Emily turned up the radio. "Just to drown you out."

She drove in silence as Sue fell asleep.

Emily glanced across at Sue. Her skin was pale and a large rash
covered her upper arm. Her legs were thinner and she seemed
restless in her sleep. Emily turned away as the steep descent to the
Spit Bridge opened before her.

"Ridiculously beautiful." She murmured to herself as the car
descended the hill. Low green hills, blue water, white hulled yachts,
cream sand converged together in simplicity. Moreton Bay figs

swept to the ground, in a chivalrous bow to visitors. The slow, beach rhythms of Manly. Surfer and sea, locked together in languid motion, awaiting the defining wave of the day.

Sue dug her toes into the sand and gazed as people strolled past. "Look, Emms, all these separate lives, converging here today. We walk the shore, our hearts caught up in our own affairs, indifferent to what lies in other hearts. Amazing, no?"

Emily nodded.

"You've always been my quiet buddy." Sue nudged her. "What's he like, the Egg King?"

Emily laughed. "Gerald? A bit like Bob, authoritarian, decisive, money driven. Soulless."

"Attractive traits for some."

"Once." Emily stretched her legs out. "I miss my quiet walks with Mimi. Wherever I turn nowadays, I crash tackle into a bloke with an opinion of me."

"Tell them to piss off."

"That's not my nature"

" I'd been so rude if any bloke tried it with me. They would exercise their mangy dog in Penrith to avoid me."

Emily smiled. "Underneath the bluster, Gerald's running from his age, his divorce, his loneliness."

"Your tolerance levels are higher than mine. You may yet become the Egg Empress."

"I knew that was coming."

"The Chicken Chatelaine."

"Cruel but funny."

Sue lifted a sea shell. "Small, perfect thing, flung by tidal waves, held in children's hands, discarded."

"Why so philosophical today?" Emily took her shoes off and stretched out on the sand. "That's so nice."

Sue stared at the horizon. "I'm back at work in ten days, surrounded by unsaid words. Do you think you'll live beyond five years? What's it like facing a life threatening illness? Did you change? Yes I did, but no one will ask me that." She shrugged her shoulders. "I'll go back to corporate words."

"I'll ask you, Suzie."

"But you won't tell me your secrets."

"Do we have to go there again?"

"We never did." Sue stared at her. "I've known you forty years but I don't really know you. We live within walls and we never walk beyond them. I could die today and say I never knew another person intimately. That's not much to summarise a life with, is it?"

Emily nudged her. "Sounds like you're considering the NGO position."

Sue shrugged. "I've not thought about it."

A wave broke on the shore and foam rushed towards them. Laughing children scrambled around them, screaming as they clutched buckets and spades.

"They're learning boundaries now," Sue murmured, "never show fear, live blindly in the moment."

"Suzie," Emily bent her head towards her. "I thought I would die many times when I was a child. When Dad hit Mum, I knew he could kill her. She was the only thing that stood between him and us. I've faced death too."

They held hands as she spoke. "It was better when he was drunk, the beatings wouldn't last as long. We'd hide under bedcovers to muffle the sounds. Mum never cried out, she didn't want us or the neighbours to hear. He was careful, he'd attack her silently. They both played the game so well."

"Did you ever tell Bob?"

"No! He came from another world, a happy childhood world. He still doesn't know. When we were together, I was shielded from those memories. Of course they came back, in my dreams, in my thoughts. I couldn't shake the fear."

"Your poor mum."

"It was better when he left her for good. He'd been drinking more and more. One day, he didn't come home. Mum called me, my kids were still small. She was frantic. Said she was afraid something had happened to him. I nearly laughed, I hoped he was dead. He never came back."

"That's when you told me they'd separated."

"Yes. I saw him once in town, he was living on the streets. I had Dominic with me and I crossed the road and hid my face. Thank God he didn't see me. The police let us know when he died. He carried his license with him always, I guess that made him feel a part of the world still." Emily looked out to sea. "I called Rodney to tell him. He hung up on me."

"Why?"

"He was still angry I didn't back him up the night he fought with Dad. Rod was punching Dad, blood was everywhere. Mum was begging him to stop, I was begging him. He shouted he was doing it for her, for all of us. I'll never forget the look in his eyes at that moment, like we were complete strangers to him. In the end, Dad took everything away from us, even our love for each other."

"That's a dreadful burden to carry."

"I just felt embarrassed. We were never good enough for him. I learned to creep quietly as a child, or I'd trigger a violent mood-swing. My mind was trained to diffuse his moods, if he was happy, I was. If he was angry, I became invisible."

"Why did he hit you that time?"

"I answered him back. Rodney hadn't been gone long and I was lost without him. No one to form a barrier against the constant stress. He hit me hard, so he knew I'd never step out of line again. I didn't. That man's cruelty made me a lifelong servant."

"You weren't in school the whole week. I tried calling but there was no answer."

"We stayed in the Blue Mountains with Mum's cousins. The bruises were awful and I was ashamed. The biggest problem my friends had was boys and pimples and I was black and blue." Emily dug her toes in the sand and watched the fine grains separate and fall back to the shore line. "We ran away. He didn't know where we were." She laughed. "This will sound strange but it was a wonderful week. It was windy and wet, we sat in front of a wood fire at night and read books. I could concentrate on the words, I was so relaxed. I still remember the teen magazine I read, the cute articles on pop stars. I imagined what it must be like to always be so relaxed. I prayed we could live there always, I felt so free. Mum was programmed to his violence, I guess she felt it was her duty to go back to him. The lessons you learn at your mother's knee, huh?"

Sue was silent. She gripped Emily's hand and stared out to the Pacific. The beach had cleared in the early evening, save a collection of surfers turned to the horizon, their backs arched, awaiting the last curl before darkness fell.

Chapter 37

"Sylvia, what lovely flowers! You shouldn't have." Emily sat at the kitchen table and held the bouquet in her hands.

"I wanted to thank you for the tickets. Must've seemed very ungrateful but I was all jumbled up inside."

"I'm glad you enjoyed it."

"I didn't say that. Afterwards, I was exhausted for a week. Seeing Dulcie again threw me."

"She's very sweet."

"On the surface, she's a layer of pure sugar. But she can needle you. Age hasn't changed her."

"Her grandson was lovely."

Sylvia nodded. "She was blessed with good family. Her husband died years ago, she probably talked him into an early grave. He barely spoke, he was that quiet. Death must've been a respite for him."

Emily laughed. "When did you meet her?"

"When we first moved here. She's from the country as well, but bred garrulous. She felt the need to spill every inch of her life. Every kick during her four pregnancies, every sleepless night with her toddlers. She was St Dulcie, crucified by her home duties. Had plenty of time to remind me that I could organise the church fetes, because I had no family to tend to. But that was a lifetime ago. What's your news?"

"I have both children at home again. My daughter has moved in."

"Not another heartbroken child?"

"Heartbroken in a different way. Not falling pregnant has unsettled her and made her re-think her life."

"Let her follow her instincts. No one knows what a woman feels in that situation." She waved her hand. "What else is new with you?"

"Well, my girlfriend isn't returning my calls."

"The sick one?"

Emily nodded. "We always text or call each other but nothing in ten days."

"Is she cross with you?"

"I think so."

"Then just say sorry and be done with it."

"I think she feels betrayed by me. I'm not good at talking about myself."

"I've noticed that." Sylvia's sharp eyes focussed on her. "I don't know much about you yet."

"Not much to say. I look after people, that's what I do."

"You'll want more," Sylvia remarked, "everyone wants to be loved and appreciated."

"Some of us are happy to go about unnoticed."

"And that fulfils you, my girl?"

"No."

"Then why do it?"

"Because it's all I know."

"You've short-changed your life. You don't want to look back and feel you've squandered time."

"That's easy for you to say. Your family were normal, they treated you well. I grew up with an alcoholic father and my nerves were permanently damaged. Every decision I made in my life reflected the fear that man inspired. I looked for danger everywhere, were my babies safe at night, was my husband laughing behind my back? Was I really worth so little? I knew inside my heart I was, I was raised to believe it." She caught her breath. "So don't lecture me."

Sylvia stood and moved across to the sink. "Let's have a cup of tea, it soon rights the world." She limped over to the kettle and steadied herself on the bench.

Emily noticed the walking stick resting against the table. "Are you still using the cane?"

"Unfortunately. I didn't bounce back after the last fall. Not made of rubber like I used to be."

Mimi whined and stood beside her. Sylvia stooped to pat her. "She's getting to be a proper sook, won't leave me alone most days." She hesitated. "If you feel obligated to walk Mimi, please say so. I can pay a neighbourhood child or a dog walker to do it."

"I did, initially." Emily flushed. "But I've met some interesting people because of her. We mates now, aren't we, Mims?" The dog walked across to her and nuzzled into her lap.

Sylvia nodded. "There's something about a dog, isn't there? Even for you, with your sinuses and all."

"I didn't tell you the truth about our family dog. I didn't show it but I just adored her. She was my little mate, she got me through some very hard times."

Sylvia stacked the tray and motioned with her hand. "If you would."

Emily lifted the cane. "If you would."

"If I must." Sylvia muttered. She progressed slowly up the hallway, as Emily stood behind her.

They sat on the sunny porch. A potent aroma of aged wood and flowers carried in the fine breeze.

"Glorious day," proclaimed Sylvia, "who'd be dead for quids?" She threw her cane to the floor. "You're still young. You must train your mind to be strong, and not be impeded by obstacles."

"Fighting words."

"Life's a fight, isn't it? John Edward and I started out with nothing to our names. Even in the war years, he could see the way clearing for us. We were life mates and he was my captain. I'm sorry you didn't have that."

"I don't know if any woman has that today." Emily frowned. "I don't know if my daughter has." She watched as a robin pecked at blades of grass on the lawn.

"My friend believes that I hid my life from her." Emily accepted the cup of tea. "but I didn't know how to share. I was so ashamed of my family, I never spoke of them. I bet my brother never has either."

"Do you keep in touch?"

Emily shook her head.

"Call him. When the world turns on you, family is all you have. They are your roots, the stock you come from."

"I'll see."

"You'll do well to mark my words."

"Yes, ma'am."

Sylvia laughed. "I'll stop there. I'm getting my 'Sylvia has spoken' tone. John Edward called me the oracle when I did that! Funny man." She sipped her tea. "In my day, we kept quiet if there was a family problem. I had an uncle who liked a drink and my dad kept an eye on him at social functions."

"Did he beat his wife unconscious too?"

Sylvia shook her head. "I'm sorry."

"I'm turning you into an apologist. Tables turning now."

They laughed.

"What became of him?"

"My dad? Died a homeless drunk. I didn't care but Mum was distraught. I think she felt a failure all over again, he preferred to live rough than stay with her. Mean bastard."

"Your kids must've been terrified of him."

"Barely knew him, don't remember him. I never told them about my childhood, too big a burden for little shoulders. They think I'm naturally neurotic."

Sylvia laughed. "Shame your husband didn't steer you to clear waters."

"Yes." Emily drained her cup and poured herself another tea. "I craved a family and safety, not romance. Life's a trade and I traded big time."

"We all make them." Sylvia spoke softly. "I used to hide in my house from 3pm to 4pm on a weekday. Couldn't bear the sound of children walking home from school. I would hear them laughing, skipping with their ropes, splashing in their gumboots in the rain. I waited until all the sounds passed by, then I would open my windows again." She leaned back in her chair. "I watched the faces of my neighbours change as they raised their children. The delicate,

Irish lass across the road became skin and bones but the love and devotion on her face made her even more beautiful. I envied her." She paused. "Dulcie would drop by unannounced with her kids some days after school for a chat. She knew it hurt me. Finally, I learnt to lock the house up, pretend I wasn't home. She got the message."

Emily was silent. She watched Sylvia's eyes. Alternate fierce and tender lights lit them.

"I must be getting old." Sylvia mused. "That's not something I'd usually tell someone. What a grumble I've had! And such a blessed life to boot. Mother would be ashamed of me."

"Thank you for telling me. I feel privileged."

Sylvia was silent, lost in the past, her eyes tender and sad.

Emily stood quietly and cleared the table. She stacked the tray and walked down the hallway to the kitchen.

Sylvia sat and watched the sunlight shift on the lawn, Mimi by her side.

…......................

The last of the sunlight faded on the lounge floor. Emily watched as dusk descended. She held the chalk and wrote in a slow hand:

"Do we ever truly know someone? Or are our words censored, to the point where we don't exist at all?"

Chapter 38- View 4

"Not a long walk, Mims." Emily bent to unleash the impatient dog. "I start work earlier today. Serena needs the morning off, she's got an interview somewhere." She stepped on the soil and the scent of fallen leaves embedded in the earth arose. Winter scents. "Go girl, the park is ours."

She watched as Mimi sprang ahead, sinewy joy in every bound.

Across the park, a figure emerged from his sports car. As he strode across the green, the familiar set of his shoulders and swing in his walk caught at Emily's heart.

"The kids said you'd be here." He bent to kiss her cheek. "Looking good, Emmy."

"And you, Bob." She raised an eyebrow. "7am is an unusual time to visit."

"If I don't collect the teak oil before the weekend, Elspeth will kill me."

"Bunnings all out, huh?"

He didn't reply. He nodded to the park and surrounding street "Good area, your flat should hold value here."

"Thanks."

"How was your holiday?"

"Amazing. Elspeth bought some great clothes."

"Did she learn to cook to your satisfaction?"

"Don't be sarcastic, Emmy, it doesn't suit you. She cooked fine before. I just needed a break from brown rice."

"Lots of casseroles and soup now."

He scowled.

"Didn't work, huh?"

"She said it was too fattening."

"That's what happens when you marry someone with a washboard stomach."

"You shouldn't go at Elspeth like that, it's unfeminine."

"Really, and sleeping with someone else's husband is?"

"Don't be bitter. It's such a waste of energy."

"Stop telling me what to be. If you do that to the new wife, she'll dig her manicured claws in."

"Elspeth has a strong sense of who she is. You never did. You were always checking on the kids, or your mum. That old bitch never did anything for you."

"She saved my life."

"What! Speak up, Emmy."

"All those years together and I never shared one memory with you." She thought. "And I never will." She spoke. "It's Emily. Why are you here, Bob?"

"The teak oil."

"Then wait till I'm finished." She walked away and threw a ball in the air. "C'mon girl, go catch."

Mimi collected the ball in a messy lick of fur and jowly teeth.

"Good girl! Now again." She threw the ball further and Mimi raced across the grass.

Emily glanced backwards. Bob sat on a bench, texting on his phone. She hid a smile and turned away.

"Good girl. And again."

"I have to go to work."

"Nearly done."

"One last throw, girl." Mimi barked as the ball flew in the air.

"Make her stop that barking," Bob stood, "before she sends me deaf."

"You're becoming sour in middle age. I thought the 38 year old would keep you cheerful."

"I'll meet you at the flat." He turned and walked to the carpark.

She continued her leisurely walk. "We won't hurry for him, Mims."

Sylvia waited on the porch, leaning over the railing as Emily opened the front gate.

"There's a man standing in your front lawn. Looks suspicious to me."

Emily snorted. "Tall and dark haired?"

Sylvia nodded.

"I know him."

"Which one of the park crowd is he? The egg millionaire?"

"The ex husband."

"Looks like a scoundrel."

"Is a scoundrel. I think he wants something from me. See you for afternoon tea tomorrow."

Sylvia patted Mimi. "Come, girl. We'll send up a prayer and a woof for Emily."

Bob sat on the bench near the fountain, jacket slung over his shoulders. "She looks ancient. Has she got family?"

"Lots in Adaminaby."

"Where on earth is that?"

"NSW snow country."

"We only ski in New Zealand."

Emily ground her teeth. "I've only got a few minutes, I have an early start today." She hesitated at the security door.

"Don't want to show me inside, huh? I told you we should've waited to sell."

Emily pushed at the door and ran up the stairs.

He whistled as she opened the front door. "You can tell Dom's living here! I knew I made a good call when I said no to him."

Emily was silent as she searched the upper shelves of the hall cupboard. She stood on tiptoe and felt at the back of the shelf. "Please be here." A tin just within her reach. "Yes!" she muttered.

She re-entered the lounge to see him sitting on her leather sofa.

"God, I wish you took the old stuff. I love this modern look. Elspeth is forever dusting the furniture and china. It's like living in a doll's house."

"I used to have that job. She's welcome to it."

"If you don't want some of these paintings, I'll take them off your hands."

"It's a long story."

He leaned on the armrest. "Must be cramped with the kids."
"We manage."

Emily picked up her phone and dialled.
"Can't you do that later? I can't stay long."
"You can wait, Bob." She turned away. "Sue, I was hoping I'd hear from you this week. What news? That's brilliant! So, all clear?"
"Emms, you sound really brittle. Is everything ok?"
"Bob's over for a visit."
Silence on the phone.
"He needed my teak oil."
"I hope you poured it up his ..."
"Gotta go. Talk soon."
Bob motioned with his head. "What's with the chalk board?"
"Sue gave it to me."

"Say no more." He stared at the ground as he spoke. "Elspeth's pregnant."
"Oh."
"That's it, no congratulations?"
"Are you happy?"
"She's thrilled"
"Are you equally thrilled?"
"I know what's coming. It's a boy, so we'll need to move to a house someday. I'll be sixty when he starts school."
"And over eighty when he finishes uni."
"Are you seeing anyone?"
"Several men."
"You're being facetious."
"Yes. At least you'll be a younger dad than Rupert Murdoch."
"You're laughing at me." He looked down at the floor again. "Are the kids leaving soon?"
"Dom's found a flat, he moves in a fortnight. Sarah's sharing with friends for now. She's thinking things through with Matt."
"Both those bloody kids can't hold a partner down. I don't know

where we went wrong with them."

He looked directly at Emily. "I could use some time away from home. We're fine but I need to get my head around this situation."

"Stay with her while you do. She's hormonal, you need to be there for her."

"I don't want to do it again. I should be having grand-kids but those kids of ours can't settle down. I'll have to produce the offspring."

"It's your choice, Bob."

He stood abruptly. "Sorry to see the place looking so overrun." He stared at her intently. "You used to have such gentle eyes. Now they're hard and bitter. I'll see myself out."

Emily watched him leave, wordless. Then she walked across to the chalkboard and rubbed out the existing words and wrote: "I gain a 4th view of me: bitter eyes. A small life begins and something ends." She placed the chalk down and filled the kettle, her hands completely steady.

Chapter 39

Emily wiped her palms against her shorts. She dialled the number and her heart rate increased as she entered the digits. "I should hang up," she thought, "he'll have moved away by now."

"Hello." The slow, deep voice she loved as a girl.

She swallowed. "Rodney, it's Emily."

"My God, is Bob dead?"

She laughed.

"The kids OK?"

"Yes."

A pause and then silence. She searched for easy words, none came.

"I'm ringing to say hello." She stumbled on. "I've wanted to call you more regularly since we lost Mum."

She cleared her throat, waiting for his words.

"Please speak," she silently prayed, "take my awkwardness away with your beautiful voice."

He remained silent.

"I just thought it would be nice to talk occasionally. It's just the two of us now."

Her throat constricted and she fought to keep her voice even. "Mum was always sorry we lost touch. She blamed herself for the split. Said she wasn't worth either of us."

"She was a very humble woman."

Emily closed her eyes and pressed her forehead against the wall. Her throat completely blocked, her eyes streamed tears. She wiped them on her sleeve, to no avail. They continued.

"For a woman who's called to talk, you're being remarkably silent."

She laughed, coughing tears simultaneously.

"You did that as a kid," his beautiful voice continued, "if we were upset about Dad, Mum would tickle you, remember? You'd laugh and cry at the same time. She loved it, said you were so innocent in your emotions."

Emily's throat caught again. "We don't have many happy memories, do we?" she murmured.

"We don't have any, Emmy Lou."

"I haven't heard that in years, Rod! You were fascinated by that singer. Did you ever see her in concert?"

"Several times in the city."

"I wish I'd known, I could have gone with you."

"I needed to be away."

"I know. We lost so much, didn't we. Our family, our memories." She hesitated. "Did you want to see Mum before she died?"

"No," he sighed and she pressed the phone closer to hear him. "I wasn't ready, I was still so angry with both of them. When I left home, I had no social skills, no ability to cope with the outside world. I blamed her for not leaving him for our sake. For the past eighteen months, I've done counselling, more for anger management than anything."

"I'd be a prime candidate for that."

"Depends where you are with forgiveness. You seemed to have forgiven Mum years ago. I never could. Once I let go of that, I changed."

"That was because I had kids. They made me see how hard it was for Mum. She was trapped by poverty and a poor education. She had nowhere to go."

"I know. No one in the family stepped in, so we were left to suffer his madness."

"Have you forgiven him?"

"Not even trying."

She laughed. "Can't say I think of him kindly either."

A lull in words. Emily leaned against the kitchen wall.

"Sue hardly speaks to me now."

"Who?"

"Sue Smith. You would know her from high school."

"The short, bossy blonde who told me I had crap taste in music?"

"Her."

"My God, that's a long friendship. I've never had one. Never let anyone get that close."

"The same is true of me. I never told Bob the truth about Dad."

"At least you married, had a family."

"Now divorced and living on my own."

"I'm sorry, I didn't know."

"We don't share in this family."

"How long ago, Emmy Lou?"

"Beginning of the year. My New Years resolution was to be happy."

"And your success rate?"

"Near zero."

A low laugh. Emily's eyes pricked again and she wiped them on her sleeve.

"Anyway, that's not really true. I have realised how much I love my kids, how lucky I am to truly love someone."

"We didn't have that privilege."

"There was no time to feel it. There was no safety in our lives."

He was silent.

"And if Sue forgives me, I have one good friend. I never told her either and it hurt her badly."

"Kids aren't meant to suffer those heightened emotional states."

"And yet children all over the world are exposed to it."

He was silent.

"Rod, I always wanted to apologise for not standing up to him that night too. I've never forgiven myself."

"You were a kid. I never forgave myself for abandoning you and Mum. My anger was my excuse not to go back."

"Where to from here?"

"I'll call you," he replied, "we'll talk some more. Give me your phone number."

"Wait a sec, I have to look it up. I never call myself." She flicked through an notepad. "Are you there, Rod? OK, write this down."

She placed the phone in the receiver and the notepad on the

bench. From the back pages, a torn photo fell out.

Two golden haired children smiled out from the black and white image. A boy had his arm around a young girl's shoulder. He gap toothed smile turned adoringly towards him.

"That's us, Rodney," she thought, "two lost children, who'll spend their lives looking for the way back home."

Chapter 40

"Sylvia, I'm honoured that you've come over."

"If truth be told, my girl, curiosity got the better of me."

Sylvia perched on the leather sofa. Her legs didn't reach the floor. Her eyes darted about the flat and absorbed the Spartan lines of the design.

"She looks ancient," Emily reflected, as she busied herself with the kettle, "like a sun-dried raisin."

Sylvia clasped her hands and the sweet gesture smote Emily's heart.

"Did you run out of money while decorating?"

Emily laughed. "No, just interest."

"You look like someone who'd display china in cabinets and tapestry on the walls."

"In my previous life, I did."

"Do you still miss it?"

"Less and less, thanks to you and Mimi."

Sylvia clapped her hands as Emily approached with a tray. "Oh, you do serve tea nicely. I won't be able to use my old things when you visit again."

Sylvia's cheeks were flushed.

"She's uncertain," Emily mused, "outside of the gentle rhythms of her day." She held out a plate. "Help yourself, Sylvia."

The tiny, blue veined hand sought a biscuit and retreated quickly. "What would Mimi give for a nibble of this?"

"I'll give you a selection for Her Highness." She sighed. "My kids are leaving at the end of the month."

Sylvia raised an eyebrow.

"Don't get me wrong," Emily continued, "I'll enjoy the space again. But they warmed this place, Dom on his laptop, sprawled on the couch. Sarah on the floor, texting Matt, her feet curled over Dom's legs. Made me feel less like I'd raised a warring tribe and more like two loving adults. I stopped feeling homesick for my old life."

"Even if you were unhappy in it?"

Emily nodded. "Now, did the plumber fix the leak?"

"Yes," Sylvia leaned forward, "it's highway robbery how much he charged. Told me it was half his usual price. Imagine!"

Emily laughed. "Plumbers are the new doctors." She motioned to the walking stick. "Is it a constant now?"

"Unfortunately. Seems like one good knock was all I needed to tame me for good."

"Amazing what one good knock can do."

Sylvia reached for her handbag. "I've brought you something." She twisted the old fashioned clasp and lifted a small, wrapped package to Emily. "It's to thank you for walking Mimi. And so much more."

"No need, Sylvia. I've enjoyed it enormously, it helped settle me into the neighbourhood. I've even enjoyed your cantankerous company."

"Well, keep it. I won't take it back."

"Thank you." Emily removed the tissue paper cover, to reveal a jewellery box. She lifted the lid. "Oh, Sylvia, I can't take this, it's too valuable." She lifted a silver locket from the satin bed. "Bob's mum had one just like it, from her grandmother."

"So you already have one?"

"No, that old biddy hated me. Snake hips has it now." Emily looked at Sylvia. "Don't you have family you want to pass it down to?"

"They'll get everything I have. My nephew will invest my estate into the land. A very sensible man, I've plenty of time for him."

"I love it!" Emily lifted the locket in the air. "You've polished it for me." She gently opened the clasp. Inside the glass case, a wisp of white hair lay encircled.

"It belonged to my grandmother. She favoured me, said I was the apple of her eye. It came from England, that's all I know about it. You can have it valued at a jewellers, they know about such things."

"I know its value already." Emily fingered the small locket. "It's priceless to me." She motioned to the hair. "From John Edward?"

Sylvia nodded. "Yes." She sat back and Emily noticed her pallor.

"Are you feeling OK?"

"If I could have a glass of water."

"Oh, sorry, of course. No, stay there, I'll get it."

Sylvia sat back on the sofa, her feet rising in the air as she did so.

"You've been doing so well. Not a sorry in weeks until now."

"I was mortified you'd pass out in my apartment." She held out the glass. As she did so, the locket clinked the glass and Sylvia started.

"You won't remove the hair, will you?"

"That's the last thing I'd do."

"It won't feel strange wearing it around your neck?"

"I'll never take it off."

"Thank you, it's all I have… If I were to die tonight, no one would remember them. I hoped you would."

Emily gently held the locket. "I will. It's a lovely gift, thank you."

Sylvia rubbed her hand along the cold leather seat as she spoke. "This is what it must be like to have a daughter. Visits to the Opera, afternoon tea, warm chit chat. I've loved it. Thank you."

She looked at Emily. "If I had a daughter, the locket would have been hers. I'm glad it yours now."

She was quiet and Emily stood. "I'll top up the pot."

"No, please, I must get home." Sylvia tried to stand and Emily held out her hand.

"Let me help, the leather is quite slippery."

"Indeed. I feel like Alice falling down the rabbit hole."

Emily laughed. "I'll see you home."

"Thank you." Sylvia stared at the locket as she reached for her cane.

"It suits you." She walked slowly to the front door, hunched over her cane.

Emily noticed her increased frailty.

The climb down the stairs left Sylvia breathless.

Emily's concerned face made her laugh.

"I won't die on you," she muttered, "I have too much pride to die in a public place."

"Good," Emily replied, "my neighbours find me deeply suspicious as it is. That'd be the icing on the cake."

She opened the security door and Sylvia walked onto the lawn. "That's a funny little fella, if ever I've seen one." She pointed her cane at the statue. "Imagine carving something that spouts water from there." She chuckled to herself. "John Edward and I had some good laughs in Italy over some of the fountains we saw. So much nakedness, they're mad for it. No wonder they elected Berlusconi."

She walked slowly to her front gate. "Thank you for understanding my gift." She reached over to Emily and held the delicate locket in her hands. "It was my comfort for many years. It suits you, much more so than that flat does and your silly neighbours. You deserve better, my girl."

Before Emily could reply, Sylvia opened the gate latch and walked up the garden path.

Emily thought she saw her brush her eyes as she climbed the porch stairs.

She walked back to the complex, stopped at the fountain and bent down to the cherub. She traced her hand over its face. The sweet, chubby features were a sharp contrast to the marble's cold touch.

"What are you doing?" A voice boomed above her and Emily started.

Rhonda peered over her balcony, dressed in a flowing caftan.

"Just admiring the repair job Luigi did. The joins don't show at all." The triple chins glared at her.

Emily stood and walked quickly back inside.

Chapter 41

"Elegant choice." Emily smiled at her children.

Sarah looked up from the menu. "I don't know what to have, the corn fed chicken or salted salmon."

"It all sounds expensive."

"Relax, Mum you know it's on us."

Dominic's curls hung low over his forehead and covered his brow and long eyelashes.

"What do you think, Sar?" He pointed to a dish on the menu and she read the ingredients, her head tilted towards him. "Try it, Dom." Her smooth blond locks brushed her face and shoulders. Her intense blue eyes scanned the menu. "I think we should order the salted salmon for Mum, she'll never order anything decent for herself."

He nodded in agreement.

"You OK with that, Mum?"

Emily started out of her reverie. "Of course, as long as you don't order salt encrusted snails."

Sarah touched a waiter's arm and he bent to her calm beauty.

Emily glanced about the restaurant. White painted walls, white damask tables and long chandeliers created a refined space. White candlesticks at the centrepiece of each table, surrounded by a sprig of green leaves. She turned back to the conversation.

Dominic spoke. "That's something Elspeth would order."

"I know, she's got some weird cravings." Sarah stopped.

Emily tapped her hand. "It's OK, darling, I know."

"Good," Sarah leaned forward, "how weird is it, I'm gonna have a sibling at 26."

"Major weird." Dominic nodded. "Were you upset, Mum?"

"Good luck to them, I say. She deserves a child, she'd regret turning 40 and not starting a family."

"Good on you, Mum, that's the spirit!"

"Absolutely. We could even form a babysitting club for them. Alternate nights of the week and we could polish their furniture as a sideline. Teak oil is bloody expensive. Apparently."

"You're not OK with it." Dominic reached across to her.

"I don't know what I am." She snapped. "As long as they don't want anything from me."

"They don't."

Emily sat back. "I don't envy him. But it really pisses me off that he lands on his feet every time. The younger wife to look after him in his dotage, who I'm sure he won't cheat on because he knows he's on his last chance. I hate how it turns out so sunny for him, when he's such a conniving pig."

"Go, Mum!" Sarah laughed. "Good to hear you venting for once."

Emily leaned back in her chair. "I don't usually do that because it takes so much out of me." She glanced at the other patrons. "How did you find out about this place?"

"We came here for Dad and Elspeth's engagement party."

"Charming. If I'm really lucky, they'll drop by tonight."

"They won't, I told them we're coming tonight."

"Co-ordinated dates, I should be flattered."

"Mum!"

Emily looked at her children. "I'm being ungracious, I know."

"Lovely pendant," Sarah reached across and fingered the locket. "I haven't seen that one."

"It's from Sylvia." Emily opened the latch. "It's got a lock of her husband's hair in it."

"Does that feel a bit weird?"

"She didn't want him to be forgotten when she's gone. Amazing love they had."

"I hope I have that one day." Sarah looked thoughtful. "I mean, I hope Matt and I can sustain that."

"Do you miss him?"

"So much. But I can't go back yet. I love being with my mates again in Sydney. They're my world, as much as he is. I don't know if he fully understands."

"Maybe not, Sar, but he loves you enough to wait."

Sarah's eyes filled with tears and Dominic handed her a tissue. "Practically new, I only blew my nose once on it."

She pushed it away. "God, I look awful when I cry." She tried to smile as she wiped her eyes. "What if he finds someone else while I'm still deciding?"

"Sarah, if your heart is telling you to stay in Sydney for now, there's a reason. You may not know why, but obviously you need time to process things."

"But I'm not that person," Sarah wiped her eyes again, "I always know what I want."

"Unlike me." Dominic smiled.

"Every time I decide to go back the next weekend, something stops me. Like there's a string that pulls me from taking the next logical step to my life. God, I'm turning into you, Dom. It's not fair." She blew her nose on the tissue. "I'll get a disease from sharing this."

"We love you, Sar. Dysfunctional cow that you are."

"Stop it, Dom." She laughed. "Mum, did you love Dad passionately?"

Emily shook her head. "I loved him carefully. I've only ever loved you, Dom and Sue passionately."

"Is she in touch?"

"One phone call in 5 weeks. I've realised recently that she's my cornerstone in life. She's always loved me, even if your dad didn't. Sue feels I've been dishonest with her over the years."

"But you're the soul of honesty, Mum."

"By omission." She looked at her children. "Did I ever tell you that your grandfather was an alcoholic?"

"No."

"That he beat Grandma black and blue?"

They shook their heads.

"That he beat me once so badly, Mum and I escaped to the Blue Mountains for a week so my school wouldn't call the police when they saw me?"

They stared at her, stunned.

"That Uncle Rodney left because he couldn't take the violence any more?"

Sarah held her hand to her mouth.

"I even left your Dad once, for all of five minutes. I walked out of the house and took off on foot down the Boulevard. On my way, I saw a stalled, old model Holden with a women and and her two kids inside. I could almost smell her poverty and desperation. I turned around and walked back home." She laughed drily. "That's when I started to pack things away in the attic. Everyday things we'd need, for the day I was ready to leave. Just like my mum, squirreling things away for her escape."

Emily twirled her wine glass. "So you see, our friendship was based on a lie. I only told Sue the small things of my life because the big, defining moments hurt so much." She leaned over and held onto Sarah and Dominic's hands as she spoke. "So if your hearts hesitate in love, listen to the words that are too painful to express. They're the ones that define who you are." She wiped her eyes.

"The truth is, the loss of my friendship with Sue hurts more than the divorce. I never saw it coming."

Sarah leaned over and held her hand tight. "We love you, Mum. Always will. I'm sure she does too. Give it time."

"Thank you." Emily pulled a face. "How are my eyes, Sarah? And my nose, pink like a pig?"

Sarah nodded. "Genetic trait, obviously."

They laughed.

"Oh no!" Dominic looked across the restaurant. "Act happy, everyone. Dad and Elspeth just walked in."

"Bugger." Emily gritted her teeth. "OK, I haven't been crying, I have a cold."

Sarah flicked her hair back. "Act delighted, like I've just told you the most amazing news."

"Really?" Emily blew her nose loudly.

"No," Sarah whispered, "just act it."

Emily re-applied her lipstick. "Have they seen us?"

"Just now," Dominic waved, "wow, she doesn't look pregnant, just heaps thinner."

"She won't in four months." muttered Emily, smoothing her hair.

"Hello."

They turned at the sound of Bob's voice. "I didn't know you'd booked a late meal. This is our regular time."

"Bob." Emily forced a smile.

"And this is Elspeth."

She forced a bigger smile. "Hello. I've heard your delightful news. Congratulations."

"Thank you." Elspeth's voice was well modulated. "If only the nausea would leave, I could start enjoying the pregnancy."

"Oh, if not nausea, it could be piles, or cramps or swelling. You could end up looking like the Goodyear balloon. Be grateful for nausea." Emily smiled. "You'll have to put a bomb under Bob if you think he'll wake during the night for the baby. He couldn't do it for our kids. I can't see a quarter of a century on there'll be any improvement." She tapped the table nervously as she spoke and Dominic placed his hand over hers. "Here's our meal. Best you feed Elspeth as soon as you can, Bob, or she'll be awake all night with heartburn."

Emily watched as they walked away in silence.

"Do you think they'll invite me to the christening?"

Sarah and Dominic burst out laughing.

Emily bent over to her food. Seated between her two children, she ate with relish.

Chapter 42

"Mum, wake up!"

Emily rolled over in bed. "Shh!"

"Did you hear the phone just now?"

"Too much champagne last night." She groaned.

"You got a call from Royal Prince Alfred Hospital. Sylvia's been hospitalised."

She sat up. "What time is it?"

"Just after 5am."

"Oh my God," she swung her legs out of bed, "did she fall again? I knew I should've dropped by yesterday afternoon. She seemed out of sorts this week."

"She's asked for you." Dominic turned on the bed light. "I'll drive you there."

"No need," she groped for the locket and placed it around her neck as she headed to the bathroom. "I'll make my own way. Thanks, son." She kissed him. "I had a wonderful time last night."

She ran out the front door and down the stairwell. The security door was ajar and she felt a prickle of concern. As she stepped on the lawn, her shoes filled with water. "Oh, yuck!" She lifted her foot. "It's soaked! Bloody fountain's leaking again." She squelched across to the fountain and peered down. "Oh my God!" She felt in the dark for the cherub and encountered a jagged stump.

Above her, a balcony light switched on. Rhonda and her three chins appeared over the railing. "Who's down there? Show yourself."

Emily froze. Then bolted to the carpark, her legs trembling as she ran. Her sandshoes made a sucking sound on the concrete. She flung herself into her car and accelerated to the security door. "Please God," she prayed, "let her not be waiting for me. If you really exist, do me this one favour."

Rhonda stood in the driveway, waving a torch light.

Emily slowed her car and wound down her window.

"It was you all along."

"It's not what you think."

"Really, just a coincidence, huh?"

"Please move, I have to see a friend in hospital, it's urgent."

"Oh, Emily, that's so pathetic."

"Rhonda, move your fat arse or I'll flatten it for you."

"You can tell you're from the western suburbs."

"That's right. Now bloody move." Emily accelerated and Rhonda shuffled aside quickly.

"Please God, may Sylvia be OK. You failed me on the Rhonda prayer, don't do it a second time." Emily felt the blood rush to her ears as she sped down the quiet street. Traffic was minimal, only late night revellers and shift workers shared the early morning roads. She reached the hospital within minutes and raced to reception.

"I'm here to see Sylvia Baker. She was admitted last night."

The young receptionist checked her screen. "She was in Emergency. Down the hall, then left at the end."

"Thank you." Emily squelched her way down the corridor, her shoes secreting water as she walked.

"Hungover and soaked," she mused, "it doesn't get more glamorous than this."

She stood in front of the Emergency Admissions window. "I'm Emily Sargent. My friend Sylvia Baker was admitted last night. She asked to see me."

The receptionist didn't react to her dishevelled appearance.

"I guess they see it all the time," Emily thought, "what's one more train wreck?"

The receptionist glanced up from her screen. "Are you family?"

Emily shook her head. "She doesn't have any in Sydney. I'm her neighbour."

"Wait near the doors over there. I'll get someone to speak to you."

Emily shivered as she stood by the emergency doors.

The flap opened and a tall, slender intern smiled at her. "I'm Linda."

She took in Emily's wet appearance. "You're leaving a trail behind you. I'll get some slip ons for your feet."

Emily followed behind as the intern strode down a corridor of the emergency unit.

She accepted the cloth slip ons and slipped them over her sandshoes. "Thank you."

Linda looked at her keenly. "We really should contact Sylvia's family first before we speak to you."

Emily stopped in her tracks. "Why?"

"We've just lost her."

Emily tried to speak but no words came to mind.

"I'm sorry." Linda pressed her shoulder. "She had a heart condition, she'd been seen by ambulance workers before. This time, her dog was howling by the gate, which alerted a unit owner next door. He rang the police."

"Is she still here?"

"Yes. Would you like to see her?"

Emily nodded, her throat constricted.

"Come." Linda held her arm as they walked to the end of the corridor. "She asked me to call you last night but there was no reply at home when I tried. We hoped you'd arrive sooner. It wasn't ten minutes ago that we lost her."

Linda led her to a small room. "She was quite the Grand Dame, wasn't she?"

Emily stared at the figure swaddled in a white sheet. "She looks so tiny."

"They all do when they get to that age." Linda smiled. "It's sad when there's no one to farewell them. She was quite distraught earlier this evening," she shook her head, "calling out to see you. I think she knew it was her time." Linda stepped back to the doorway. "I'm glad you're here. Would you like a few minutes with her?"

"Yes, please." Emily moved to the bedside.

Sylvia looked asleep, her eyelids closed.

Linda closed the door behind her.

Emily bent over to her. "You deserved better than this, Sylvia." she whispered. "You should have children and grandchildren here, weeping over the loss of irreplaceable you." She stroked her arm as she spoke. The flaky white skin felt like ancient parchment under her touch. "You meant more to me than I realised. I'm sorry I never told you." She gave a small laugh. "Wouldn't you tell me off for apologising again!"

She held the locket in her hands. "I'll keep watch over it. He won't be forgotten. Nor you, sylvan Sylvie."

She bent and kissed her still warm forehead. The sweet smell of the elderly; floral perfume and talcum powder on Sylvia's skin. The emptiness of the room felt like a reproach to Emily.

"You deserved so much more." She whispered. She held Sylvia's small hand within her own.

Chapter 43

"What's it like being back at work?"
"Mutual indifference on both sides."
"That's a bleak assessment."
"Is it?"
They were silent amidst the tumult of families at Centennial Park.
Emily hesitated. "We've always had so much to say to each other."
She thought.
"Thanks for meeting me today, I appreciate it." She finally spoke.
Sue shrugged.
"Will you stay on at work?"
"Haven't given it a thought." Sue stared straight ahead.
"My neighbour passed away."
"The old lady? What a relief for you."
"I can't say that. She was my first friend in the neighbourhood. I
don't know what'll happen to Mimi; hopefully the country family
will take her."
They sat in silence on the park bench. Children clipped past on
ponies, joggers dogged pedestrians with nimble feet. Mothers
walked prams, with measured pace and animated talk. Toddlers
squealed as they fed ducks.

Sue watched as a young mother strolled past, with long,
braided hair, flowing skirt and sandals. A toddler clapped her hand.
"I don't miss that stage." Emily murmured. "So exhausting."
"I wouldn't know."
They sat, side by side. Emily's throat caught with unsaid words.
She glanced across at Sue. Her frame thinned by the recent
chemotherapy, she seemed stooped and frail.
"I wish I could hug you." Emily thought.
"How are the park suitors, any more dates?"
Emily shook her head. "Two are good friends now."
Sue lifted an eyebrow.
"Stan and Mark."

"The attractive one?"

"I'm not ready for anything yet."

"Even fun?"

"I'm good with security and comfort. Anything outside of that frightens me."

"How strange," Sue looked into the distance, "that's where I live best. Domestic bliss frightens me, that commitment to one."

"Two sides of a coin, perhaps?"

"Maybe," Sue reflected, "maybe we never really know anyone, even ourselves."

Emily closed her eyes, to hide welling tears. The sunshine was pure and uncomplicated on her skin.

A group of children squealed past on bicycles.

"Elspeth's pregnant."

"Wow!"

"I know."

"How are you with it?"

"I'm many things, none of them good. Pissed off that he's landed on his feet again."

"He won't be saying that when a screaming baby wakes him at 2am in the morning."

Emily smiled. "She's a very capable woman. She'll take it in her lean stride, be back at work within weeks, with nanny in place."

"Better find an old and ugly one, that's all I can say."

"I think his libido's finally in check. All the brown rice has altered his DNA."

Sue nodded.

"The kids are gone."

"Now that's some good news."

"Yes and no. I love being needed, even if I'm just staring at my heartbroken children's faces over cereal in the morning. Living for me just doesn't work."

"I've done a good job of it."

They stared at the group to their right. Birthday balloons bobbed in the air, shrieks of laughter sounded as children played pass the parcel.

Emily smiled. "You must be delighted you're in the all clear."

"Of course. I'll need frequent check ups but I'm fortunate they caught it early and I can put it behind me." Sue hesitated.

"Except?"

"Except I don't know who I am anymore." She gave a small laugh. "For months, I thought I would die, prepared myself for it. Then they told me I would live, and I don't know how to. All the old patterns of my life don't fit and I don't have anything to replace them with. I'll sort it out."

"I'll stand by you."

Sue was silent.

"I called Rodney."

"What!"

"A month ago. I've wanted to for a long time."

"All this change, Emms. I feel like I'm frozen, watching people with direction and purpose march past me."

Emily squeezed her hand but Sue drew it away.

"Did he speak to you?"

"Yes. We talked briefly of our childhood, for the first time. He said he'll call me next." Emily looked directly at Sue. "Even old relationships can start anew."

Sue looked away. "Sometimes the changes within you are so great, you have to let go of your old life and construct a new one." She turned back. "Emms, can we do this in a couple of months? I need time to reflect and somehow I can't do it around people I love."

Emily turned away. Out of the corner of her eye, she saw a balloon float in the air. It rose in the sky quickly, reflecting the light. She watched as it soared into the sunlight and was no more than a speck in the sky.

Chapter 44

Emily looked at the small cluster of people as she stood at the grave site. "She'd outlived all her contemporaries." She mused.

A young girl, of no more than ten years, placed a yellow rose onto the upturned soil. A dark haired man comforted her as she turned away, sobbing.

Emily stood at a distance, careful not to intrude. A priest blessed the coffin and it was lowered into the ground.

From the corner of her eye, she watched as a solid, grey haired woman approach her. "You must be Aunt Sylvia's neighbour. I'm Ellen, her niece." She hugged her.

"I'm Emily, that's right. It's very observant of you."

"She spoke very highly of you."

"Really? She never let on."

"Aunt Sylvia never would. Straight as a die, she could make the Pope nervous."

Emily gave a wry grin. "I'm sorry for your loss. I met her at the tail end of her life but I could tell she was an amazing woman."

"And you only knew her briefly. I adored her as a child, we all did. Mum and Dad would take us to visit Aunt Sylvie and Uncle Johnny in Sydney and I'd think I'd fallen into Heaven. They were so much fun, took us to the shows in town, amusement parks, swimming pools. They never stopped. We kids lapped it up."

She stood back from Emily and reached out to touch her locket. "I'm glad she gave it to you. She always said it had to be the right person."

Emily blushed. "Do you mind? I'm happy to return it to the family, it does have John Edward's hair inside."

"You don't know?"

Emily stared at her.

"It's the baby's hair. Uncle Johnny had the nurses' cut a lock at the hospital."

Emily was speechless.

"She never told you. I guess she knew we'd meet eventually." Ellen held her arm. "Come back to the farm for a cuppa. Follow me, I'm in the blue Ford."

Two children ran across.

Emily gazed at the girl. In her curls and lithe limbs, she could see a resemblance to Sylvia. The girl smiled shyly at her and turned away.

Emily walked to the tombstone and bent down to read the inscription. She squinted against the morning sun as she read the names:

"John Edward Baker, born Gundagai 1918, died Sydney 1982.

Lily Rose Baker, entered eternal life 1966."

"Oh, Sylvia, I'm sorry," she whispered as she brushed the tombstone. "You lost everything too."

She stood and looked for Ellen, who waved to her from a short distance away.

She followed the small procession as it drove out of the cemetery. She glanced into her rear view mirror, back at the lovely setting of the cemetery. The waters of Lake Eucumbine simmered in the cool air.

The locket on her neck felt heavy. "Sue's right," she reflected, "it's too painful to expose our hearts. All we have is careful words."

She followed as the cars turned onto a main road. Small hills, rocky outcrops and bush trees. She imagined Sylvia and John Edward galloping through the bush the summer before the war.

Ahead, Ellen's car turned into a private driveway. Her husband unlatched the gate.

Emily followed several kilometres down a dirt track. Towering ghost gums lined the driveway, wild agapanthus scattered between them.

"How glorious!" She drew in her breath. "What a place to call home."

They pulled up in front of a modern homestead.

Ellen strode over. "Welcome. Meet my husband, Bob."

A tall, thickset man held her hand in a firm grip.

"I'm sorry for your loss."

"I guess Aunt Sylvie had enough of living. I don't think she was sad to go."

"No, she was brave and had strong faith. That much I knew of her."

"Ellen tells me you didn't know about the baby."

"Come inside." Ellen took hold of her arm. "No sense starting a conversation out here." She bent towards Emily. "Men are clueless about hospitality, aren't they?"

Emily entered the house and followed down a long corridor to an open plan living area. Big windows surveyed the cattle yards and pastures outside. She imagined Sylvia striding through the pastures, cattle dog at her side.

Ellen approached, cup of tea in hand.

"Aunt Sylvie never fully recovered from losing the baby. They'd tried for years for a family. She was nearly forty when she fell pregnant. They were so overjoyed, Mum said she'd never seen Uncle Johnny like that. He was convinced it was a miracle from God." She shook her head. "There were complications at the birth. They never fully explained what happened. Mum said that if you looked into their eyes at that time, you could see the sorrow of the world within."

Ellen paused.

"After the funeral, they never came back to visit here. She came once, for Uncle Johnny's funeral but she wouldn't stay overnight."

"She must have been crushed by the loss."

"Had a nervous breakdown. Uncle Johnny took long service leave and nursed her back to health. Wouldn't put her in a hospital. Mum said they sat on the porch, sometimes past midnight, silent as sphinxes in their grief."

Emily brushed her eyes and Ellen handed her a tissue.

"When she recovered, she started to do voluntary work for local migrant services. The Italian and Greek communities in the sixties, then the Vietnamese boat people in the seventies. Aunt Sylvie helped settle them into the community. She loved to be helpful."

"She never said a word."

"No, she wouldn't. Received an OA for her services, she was tickled pink by that."

"I can't imagine the pain of losing a child."

"They were proud people. She always said she'd had a blessed life and deserved her share of burdens. I didn't think she'd survive Uncle Johnny's passing but she did. Got a dog, continued her volunteering, right up until her hip replacement." Ellen smiled. "That generation born in the 1920's were amazing, resilience and grace in the face of hardship."

Emily sipped her tea. "What was John like?"

"Oh, so handsome. I was in love with him as a little girl, vowed to marry someone just like him. Then I met Bob and re-adjusted my expectations."

They laughed.

"Uncle John was quiet and charming. Had a way of looking at you like you were the only person in the room. Aunt Sylvie was a talker and he would sit beside her as she held court. Her eyes sparkled when he was near. Said she never got over the fact he loved her, a simple farm girl. She was anything but."

They were silent. Ellen got up and rifled through the bottom drawer of a cabinet. "This is them on their wedding day."

Emily peered at the black and white photo. The young man was a head taller than his bride, her curls brushed his shoulder.

"They look so young and sweet."

"She had a bouquet of yellow roses, picked from the front garden here. She loved roses." Ellen squeezed her arm. "I'll send you a copy of it."

"I'd love that."

"Bob and I will be up in Sydney next week, to clear out the house and commence probate."

"You'll take Mimi too? I've put her into boarding while I'm down here but I'll take her out as soon as I get back."

"Don't you know?"

Emily spoke. "Another surprise?"

"Apparently. Aunt Sylvie left Mimi for you. She said it would make your path easier."

"What! I live in a flat, what was she thinking?"

"She was very specific. Aunt Sylvie was very intuitive with people."

Emily's hands were shaking as she put her teacup down. "We'll talk about this further."

"I'm under instructions not to take Mimi. Aunt Sylvie said she belonged to you." Ellen stood and moved to the kitchen. "I'll just refill the kettle."

Emily fingered the locket as she stared out the window. Her thoughts churned over Sylvia's last, enigmatic gift to her.

Chapter 45

Emily sat on her balcony. She leaned her head on the railing and her eyes adjusted to the darkness. Sylvia's home was shuttered and she heard the sound of Mimi whining inside the house. "Poor little poppet," she thought, "I'll take her for a really good run tomorrow."

The bush alongside the front verandah had clusters of roses amongst its green leaves. A splash sounded below and she glanced down at the fountain. A small shape leaned over the statue. Emily rose soundlessly and ran out of her apartment to the front security door. Her heart thudded with tension as she raced outside and sprinted to the fountain. She gripped the arm of a child as he turned in surprise.

"Don't move or I'll call the police." She whispered.

"Please don't!" A young boy of no more than ten implored her. "I won't do it again, I promise."

"What are you thinking? This is damage to public property, you could get a police record."

He started to cry as she marched him to the front of the complex. "Don't come back or I'll tell the police. I'll recognise you easily." He was shaking.

"Who put you up to it? An old lady, a skinny blonde or a fat lady? Or was it a tall, nasty man?"

He stared at her, wide eyed. "I can't say, I'll get into so much trouble."

"You're already in trouble. Sit on the fence, we need to talk."

She let go of him and he slipped away and ran down the street.

"Don't come back," she shouted to him, "they're all bloody lunatics here."

She watched as he disappeared around a corner.

Mimi barked at the sound of her voice.

"It's just me, Mims." Emily thought. "I can't bring back your favourite girl." She headed back to her apartment, the scent of roses sweet in the night air.

Chapter 46- Knockout

"He looks defeated," Emily mused, "worn down by petty people."

Gus rustled his notes. "It's been an extraordinary year. We've called five special meetings to discuss that bloody fountain. I don't think I can take anymore."

Emily looked at the committee. Flossie sat on her fold up chair, knitting a baby's sweater for another grandchild.

"They breed like rabbits." She thought.

Rhonda stood, straight-backed.

"My God, she's got a new chin." Emily did a quick count. "Four now."

Emily glanced at Cecilia. She was dressed in a sequined, cocktail dress. "Another dinner party with her lower north shore friends." She thought.

Gus cleared his throat. "Before we get to the main item, I have some news. The old lady next door died a few weeks ago."

Rhonda let out an excited squeal as he continued on. "First I thought, beauty, finally we can have some peace and quiet. Then I found out that the site has been bought by developers. They're going to build townhouses, with underground garages, on the site, so we're up for at least eighteen months of building noise. Almost makes me wish she didn't die. I hope they put that whiny dog down."

Gus continued. "We need to pull the plug on the fountain, if you'll pardon the pun, Cecilia. Owners are calling our strata manager to complain about the cost of the repairs."

"About bloody time!"

"What a shame."

"Absolutely not!"

He stared at the three women who spoke.

"What do you think, dear?" Flossie poked her needles into Emily's side.

"I think we should persevere. I don't think it will happen again."

Rhonda turned to Gus and whispered. "She knows something. I told you so."

Gus spoke. "Let me summarise the current expenses. Luigi has offered to repair it at cost price, maximum $500.00. We need to connect it to the water again, say $250.00. That's on top of previous repairs and there's no guarantee it won't happen again." He spoke directly to Cecilia. "We've repaired it three times already. We've exceeded the Body Corporate's goodwill and patience."

"You've obviously decided." Cecilia sniffed.

"It's a no brainer." Rhonda replied.

"I think it's for the best, dearie," Flossie leaned forward in her fold up chair. "There's no accounting for the malice of some." Her voice dropped to a whisper. "What next, sabotaging the electricity boxes?"

"Let's take a vote." said Gus. "All those in favour of repairing and keeping the fountain, raise your hands."

Cecilia and Emily's hands shot in the air.

Cecilia stared at the others, who kept their hands by their sides.

"I see." Her eyes as icy as her pale blue dress. She held up the severed penis of the cherub. "How do you think I feel holding this?"

Rhonda spoke up. "Wistful?"

"I'll consult my solicitor. He'll send a letter to the Strata Management. I will not pay for the malice of others."

"By that, I take it you mean me." Rhonda's chins jutted out. "The only person linked to the damage was Emily and her family on three separate occasions and yet you target me continuously."

Cecilia stamped her foot. "It can't be Emily, she wouldn't say boo to a goose. Flossie can't move that fast and Gus is too dull to think of sabotage."

"And I'm not!" Rhonda bellowed. "You can stick your cherub up your arse."

"True colours, Rhonda."

"Shut up, you botoxed bitch."

Emily started to laugh, an hysterical bubble in her throat she couldn't quell.

Cecilia looked aghast, Rhonda angry and Flossie's needles practically danced with pleasure.

"Bad week." Emily giggled.

They continued to glare at her.

She turned to Gus. "This will be my last meeting. I'm resigning from the committee for personal reasons. Goodnight."

"Yeah, like malicious damage." Rhonda muttered.

Emily stood. "No, because I'm done with stupidity."

Flossie dropped her needles as Emily swept past her.

"Arrogant bitch!"

"You have to watch the quiet ones, Rhonda." Cecilia moved close to her. "You're right, there is something about her. She scared Flossie."

Emily left the garage. A light breeze cooled her face. Inside the cottage next door, she heard Mimi whining. "I'm coming, girl," she whispered, "I won't leave you."

Chapter 47

Emily stood outside the shop front window and stared at the photos on display. She braced herself, walked to the front door, then turned away and walked back to the window display. She turned to walk inside, stopped again. She moved to a seat near the shop and crossed her arms and legs in thought.

"Just do it." She rationalised to herself. She half stood as Dominic and Sarah's faces flashed before her. She sat down again.

She glanced down the street. Couples walked, arm in arm, sauntering past the stylish stores. Groups of women stood in groups, holding groceries and chatting to each other. A man walked past with his dog, a pipe clenched between his teeth. He nodded at her and Emily smiled back. The dog sniffed at her and she thought of Mimi.

"I haven't been here since I ran away with Mum, more than four decades ago." She mused. She remembered her mother's face as they took a stroll one dusky night. She had pointed to a chimney, enchanted by the drift of smoke in the air.

"That'll be me one day, love." She stroked her hand. "A fresh start in a cosy place. Mark my words."

Emily rose to her feet. Her hands were shaking as she opened the door to the real estate agency. She approached the counter.

"May I help you, Madam?"

"Yes, please. I'd like to make an offer on a house I inspected last week. It's the three bedroom cottage on View Street."

The receptionist smiled. "Take a seat, please. I'll get an agent out for you."

Emily sank into the sofa and pressed her hands together, to stop them trembling.

…......................

"You did what!" Bob shouted down the line.

"I'm calling you as a courtesy, with my new contact details. I don't need to explain myself to you."

"You've gone bloody mad, Emily. You've only been there six months. You'll regret this."

"Perhaps, but it's something I've dreamt about since I was a kid. I could never afford a house in Sydney again. Plus, I can give the kids some money."

"It's your mother's fault. I heard her talking about moving to the Blue Mountains years ago. I told her it was a fool's dream. One freezing winter and you'll change your tune and want to come back. You'll be stuck in a one bedder out west and never be able to buy back into your complex again."

"Thank God." she murmured.

"What's that? Don't laugh at me."

"I wouldn't dream of it."

"What about the kids? Where'll they stay if they're in between relationships or flats?"

"With me. Or you, Elspeth, screaming baby and teak oil. Which by the way, you can keep."

"Don't try to be smart, it doesn't suit you. I thought you'd take me in for a while, I really need some space."

"No chance, Bob. Anyway, I can't have a dog in a flat."

"You're moving because of a dog? Of all the bloody stupid..."

Emily hung up the phone and crossed Bob's name off her list.

…......................

．．．．．．．．．．．．．．．．．．．．．．

The phone line went silent.

"You there, Sarah?"

"Yes."

"What do you think?"

Pause. "If it's what you want, Mum."

"But you're not happy?"

Sarah burst into tears. "No," she tried to control her voice. "I'm happy for you but sad for me. You'll be so much further away to visit."

"Oh darling, I'll have two spare bedrooms, loads of room for grandchildren and family to visit."

"Matt and I are still apart."

"I know." Emily's throat caught. "I'm talking future options. I'm right in the village, so you can bring friends up. We can do house swaps, I can stay in your apartment and vice versa."

"You don't have to justify it to me. I'm glad for you, truly." She paused again. "Love you, Mum."

"Love you more. And longest."

They were silent, the wellspring of emotion too strong for words.

．．．．．．．．．．．．．．．．．．．．．．

"That's amazing, Mum!"

"You like it?"

"It's brilliant. I'd hate it for myself but I can see you there."

"My inner city boy. Will you visit me?"

"Of course. What did Dad say?"

"He shouted at me."

They laughed.

"You can keep Mimi."

"I know and I can have a garden. I'm going to plant vegetables."

"In pots?"

"No, in soil. Time to make changes. How are the South America plans shaping up?"

"Fully planned." He took a deep breath. "Jenny called me. She's getting married next year."

"I'm sorry."

"Don't be. I'm seeing someone. It's casual for now but she's pretty out there."

"Piercing or tattoos?"

"Both."

"Wow. But we don't judge people by that."

He laughed. "Dad will."

"Just get her to cover up in front of him."

"No, I'll ask her to do the opposite."

"Good for you, son."

"Love you, Mum."

"Love you more. And longest."

....

Emily held the phone and went to dial the familiar number. Sue's number, ingrained in her heart, a series of digits, to access memory, self and love.

She hesitated.

"This is ridiculous." She dialled the number and waited.

Sue's voice message, brief and business like sounded in her ear. She waited for the beep.

"Hey Suzie, it's Emily. I've made some changes in my life and I want to tell you about it. Call me if you'd like to know what's happening. If I don't hear from you for a while, I'll understand. God bless you, old friend."

She walked across to the chalkboard and held the chalk in her right hand. She wrote:

"I've suffered one loss too many. What I've lost, I've gained in wisdom but I wish I could have both.

One thing I do know, is that the only view of me that counts is my own.

Here's a fifth view of me: I'm strong now, strong in places where I've been broken."

....

Chapter 48

Emily looked up from her desk and saw Serena carrying a cardboard box across the room.

"Hey!"

Serena walked over slowly.

"I hear today's your last day with the company."

"I hear you're moving out of Sydney."

Emily nodded.

"Big decisions we've made."

"Feels good. How about you?"

"Same. I'll miss everyone but it's a better job, more money and responsibility." Serena dropped the box on the floor. "It's full of crap I don't need but I don't want to leave it behind. Story of my life."

"How's the extraordinary manhunt going?"

"About the same as your coffee dates."

"Surely not that bad!"

Serena shrugged. "We should go for a drink."

"Coffee?"

"Alcohol. Let's go."

Emily glanced about the office. "It's only 3'o'clock in the afternoon."

"I know, we've missed 3 hours of drinking already." Serena pulled her arm. "C'mon no one'll notice. It's Friday afternoon."

. . . .

"Where were you at my age?" Serena waved her drinking straw at Emily.

"Home with two toddlers in the suburbs." She replied. "It was a different era, I wouldn't have dreamt of buying my own flat back then."

Serena laughed.

"I misjudged you."

"Many people do. I don't care. I thought you were an uptight, middle aged bitch."

"Ouch. And now?"

"I definitely see potential."

"Thank you. About my son..."

"It's ok. I'm not often seen as daughter-in-law potential by older women. I'd have to change who I am. Who wants that?"

"He'd hurt you."

Serena sat back.

"You have different dreams. One devastated girlfriend is enough for me to see in my lifetime." Emily squeezed her arm. "I hope you find that great love, you deserve it."

Serena's eyes filled. "Thanks." She stood. "I'll get the next round."

"Scotch, please."

"You definitely have potential."

Chapter 49

"We're on holidays, Mims!" Emily patted the dog beside her on the car seat. Mimi thumped her tail.

"I know, if I had a tail, I'd do the same thing. Four days off. We're going to stay with Sylvia's family, I can't wait. Lots of sheep for you to terrorise."

Mimi's ears pricked up at the beloved name and she whined.

"I know, I miss her too."

She turned off the highway.

A luminously beautiful landscape. Fresh rain softened the bush, darkened the soil.

She pulled into the deserted cemetery. "First things first."

She opened the car door.

Mimi bounded outside and ran towards ducks skimming the shoreline of the lake.

Emily walked amongst the graves, searching for the plot.

On the tombstone, newly chiselled into the marble: "Sylvia Baker, born Yalinda 1927, died Sydney 2014. Beloved wife and mother."

She crouched down low, to brush dust from the headstone.

"Thank you for your gift, Sylvia." She whispered. "I'm absolutely terrified but I'll try to walk bravely. Wish me luck."

She laid three yellow roses on the freshly sealed plot.

One for John Edward, one for sylvan Sylvie and one for Lily Rose of a day.

www.ingramcontent.com/pod-product-compliance
Lightning Source LLC
Chambersburg PA
CBHW060150130626
46556CB00006B/2579